CONFESSIONS
OF A
WILD CHILD

Also by Jackie Collins

The Power Trip
Poor Little Bitch Girl
Married Lovers
Lovers and Players
Deadly Embrace
Hollywood Wives—The New Generation
Lethal Seduction
Thrill!
L.A. Connections—Power, Obsession, Murder, Revenge
Hollywood Kids
American Star
Rock Star
Hollywood Husbands
Lovers and Gamblers
Hollywood Wives
The World Is Full of Divorced Women
The Love Killers
Sinners
The Bitch
The Stud
The World Is Full of Married Men
Hollywood Divorces

The Santangelo Novels

Goddess of Vengeance
Drop Dead Beautiful
Dangerous Kiss
Vendetta: Lucky's Revenge
Lady Boss
Lucky
Chances

CONFESSIONS OF A WILD CHILD

Lucky: The Early Years

Jackie Collins

ST. MARTIN'S PRESS ✖ NEW YORK

This is a work of fiction. All of the characters, organizations, and events in this novel are either products of the author's imagination or are used fictitiously.

CONFESSIONS OF A WILD CHILD. Copyright © 2014 by Chances, Inc. All rights reserved. Printed in the United States of America. For information, address St. Martin's Press, 175 Fifth Avenue, New York, N.Y. 10010.

www.stmartins.com

Library of Congress Cataloging-in-Publication Data

Collins, Jackie.
 Confessions of a wild child / Jackie Collins. — First U.S. Edition.
   pages cm
  ISBN 978-1-250-05093-9 (hardcover)
  ISBN 978-1-4668-5192-4 (e-book)
  1. Fiction.   2. Orphans—Fiction.   3. Life change events—Fiction.
I. Title.
  PR6053.0425C67 2014
  823'.914—dc23

                                        2013031935

St. Martin's Press books may be purchased for educational, business, or promotional use. For information on bulk purchases, please contact Macmillan Corporate and Premium Sales Department at 1-800-221-7945, extension 5442, or write specialmarkets@macmillan.com.

First Edition: February 2014

10 9 8 7 6 5 4 3 2 1

For all you teenagers out there
who crave your freedom and independence.
Stay Lucky . . . and only time will tell . . .

Hello, Readers

She's back by popular demand! Yes, Lucky is back, her crazy, wild teenage self. So many questions have been asked about how Lucky became the woman she is today—strong, sexy, independent, smart. Well . . . I had touched upon her teenage years in *Chances*, but in *Confessions of a Wild Child*, you will get to know the real Lucky, and how the chauvinistic ways of her father, Gino, influenced her.

Confessions of a Wild Child is the full story of Lucky's coming of age—so please enjoy.

CONFESSIONS
OF A
WILD CHILD

CHAPTER ONE

How does a girl get through school stuck with the name Lucky Saint? How does a girl answer questions about her family when her mom was murdered and her dad was once an infamous criminal known as Gino the Ram?

Beats me. But if I have to, then I absolutely can do it. I'm a Santangelo after all. A freaking survivor of a major screwed-up childhood. A girl with a shining future.

Now here I am—a week before my fifteenth birthday—about to be packed off to L'Evier, which I'm informed is a very expensive private boarding school in Switzerland, so I'd better like it or else.

I am totally pissed. My brother, Dario, is totally pissed. The truth is we're all we've got, and separating us is simply not fair. Dario is younger than me by eighteen months, and I've always felt that I should look after him.

He's sensitive.

I'm not.

He's artistic.

I'm a tomboy.

Dario likes to paint and read.

I like to kick a football and shoot baskets.

Somehow our roles got reversed.

We live in a huge mausoleum—sorry, I mean house—in Bel Air, California. A house filled with maids and housekeepers and tutors and drivers and security guards. Kind of like a fancy prison compound, only our backyard features a man-made lake, a tennis court, and an Olympic-size swimming pool. Yeah, my dad has a ton of money.

Yippee! Luxury. You think?

No way. I'm kind of a loner with very few friends, 'cause my life is not like theirs. My life is controlled by Daddy Dearest. Gino the Ram. Mister "Everything I say is right, and you'd better listen or else."

It sucks. I am a prisoner of money and power. A prisoner of a father who is so paranoid that something bad will happen to me or Dario that he keeps us more or less locked up.

So I guess being sent off to boarding school isn't such a bad thing. Maybe a modicum of freedom is lurking in my future.

However, I will miss Dario *so* much, and believe me, I know he feels the same way.

We're very different. I resemble Gino with my tangle of jet-black hair, olive skin, and intense dark eyes, whereas Dario inherited my mom's calm blondness.

Yes. I do remember my mom. Beautiful Maria. Sunny and warm and kind. Sweet-smelling with the smile of an angel and the softest skin in the world. She was the love of my father's life, even though he's had legions of girlfriends since her tragic death. I hate him for that, it's so wrong.

I miss my mom so much, I think about her every day. The problem is that my memories are akin to a frightening dark nightmare because *I* am the one who discovered her naked body floating lifelessly on a striped raft in the family swimming pool—the pool tinged pink with her blood.

I was five years old, and it's an image that never leaves me.

I remember screaming hysterically, and people running outside to see what was going on. Then Nanny Camden picked me up and hustled me inside the house. After that everything is a blur.

I do remember the funeral. Such a somber affair. Everyone crying. Dario clinging to Nanny Camden, while I clutched Gino's hand and put on a brave face.

"Don't *ever* forget you're a Santangelo," Gino informed me with a steely glare. "Never let 'em see you crumble. Got it?"

Yes, I got it. So I managed to stay stoic and dry-eyed, even though I was only five and quite devastated.

Ah, yes, fond memories of a screwed-up childhood.

Now the limo sits outside the Bel Air house, idling in our fancy driveway, ready to spirit me away to the airport.

Dario has on a sulky face—which does not take away from his hotness. My brother might only be thirteen, but he's almost six feet tall, and once he gets some freedom, girls will be all over him.

It pisses Gino off that Dario doesn't look like him. He always wanted a son—a mirror image of himself—instead he got me.

Ha-ha! I'm the son he never had.

Too bad, Daddy. Make the most of it.

Gino is sending me away to school because he's under the impression I'm a wild one. Just because I occasionally manage to escape from the house and hang out in Westwood—driving one of the house cars without a license—does not label me as wild. It's not as if I do anything crazy, I simply wander around the area checking out what it would be like to be a normal teenager. And yeah, I have to admit that sometimes I do get to talk to a boy or two.

Unfortunately, one memorable night I was pulled over by the cops, and that was a disaster. When Gino found out he went loco. "I'm sendin' you off to a school that'll drill some sense into you," he yelled, having conferred with my Aunt Jen. "What you need is an assful of discipline. I'm not puttin' up with your crappy behavior anymore. You're drivin' me insane."

That's my dad, so unbelievably eloquent.

Marco is standing next to the limo, speaking with the driver. Marco is kind of Gino's shadow and a total babe.

He's way over six feet tall, lean and muscular, with thick black curly hair and lips to die for. He's old. Probably late twenties. It doesn't matter because I have a major crush. He's handsomer than any movie star and major cool. Problem is that he talks down to me, treats me as if I'm a little kid, which I suppose in his eyes I am.

I'm on a mission to make him notice me in a different way. I want him to see me as sexy and cool, in fact everything I'm actually not.

Our guardian emerges from the house. Dario and I have christened her Miss Bossy. She's been around for three years, and has given us about as much affection as a plank of wood. She's so annoying that I can't even be bothered to hate her.

"Get in the car, Lucky," Miss Bossy says, fussing with her hair. "Dario," she orders tartly, "say good-bye to your sister, and make it quick."

Miss Bossy has been assigned to accompany me to Europe in spite of my protestations that I am quite capable of making the trip on my own. However, Gino insisted. "You go, she goes," he'd barked at me. "When she delivers you safely to the school, she leaves. That's it, no discussion."

Gino. King of the "no discussion."

Miss Bossy opens the car door and climbs inside.

Dario mouths "Jerko!" behind her back and starts kicking pebbles from the driveway toward the limo. They ping off the front of the car.

"Quit it," Marco says sharply.

Dario continues scowling. Like I said, he's not happy I'm leaving.

I run over, hug my brother, and whisper in his ear, "Stay cool, don't let 'em get you down. I'll be back before you know it."

Dario tries to keep it together, but I can see the frustration and sadness in his blue eyes; he's actually holding back tears. I feel terrible.

"C'mon, Lucky," Marco says, sounding impatient, like he really can't be bothered with this. "You don't wanna miss your plane."

Ah yes, Mister Handsome, that's exactly what I want to do.

I give Dario one final hug and blurt out, "Love ya," which of course embarrasses the crap out of him.

Dario mumbles something back, and suddenly I find myself sitting in the limo and we are off.

Gino is nowhere to be seen. He's away on a business trip.

What else is new?

CHAPTER TWO

The plane ride to Europe is endlessly long and boring. Fortunately, to Miss Bossy's annoyance, I am not seated next to her. I am seated beside a voluptuous bimbo in her forties who seems to be freaked out by flying. The woman has overbleached blonde hair and is wearing an astonishing amount of caked-on eye makeup. Her skirt is so short that it barely covers her leopard thong. I get several unwelcome flashes before she downs two Mimosas, covers herself with a blanket, and falls into a drug-induced sleep. Earlier I noted she slurped down a couple of sleeping pills with her booze. Nice. To my delight, I score a window seat, which means I don't have to bother with her. Instead I gaze out the window, thinking about Marco. Even though he escorted me to the airport, does he even realize I exist? He never speaks to me except to bark orders. He barely looks at me. Does he have a girlfriend? What does he do when he's not busy trailing Gino? What exactly is his deal?

Marco's attitude toward me sucks.

I sneak a *Cosmopolitan* magazine off sleeping bimbo's lap, and read about how to give a man the orgasm of his life.

Hmm . . . sex . . . not a subject I know a ton about. To my chagrin, I've never even been kissed—and that's because I've never spent time in the company of boys, thanks to Gino and his protective ways. Like I said—since my mom's murder, me and Dario have been kept virtual prisoners.

Oh yes—you can double-bet that I plan on making up for my life of seclusion. Indeed I do. An adventure lies ahead, and I'm totally ready to run with it.

Halfway across the ocean, sleeping bimbo awakes and immediately turns into Chatty Cathy. She starts giving me an extremely tedious rundown of her extremely boring life.

I attempt to appear interested, but it doesn't work and, halfway through her discourse on why all men are dirty dogs, I drift off into a welcome snooze.

She doesn't speak to me again.

~ ~ ~

Upon landing, Miss Bossy discovers there is another girl from Los Angeles aboard who is also on her way to L'Evier. She is a tall girl, taller than me, and I'm five-seven. She has long red hair worn in a ponytail, and a pale complexion. I hate her outfit, all neat and buttoned up, while I have on jeans and a Rolling Stones T-shirt—much to Miss Bossy's annoyance. She'd tried to get me to change before we left L.A., but I was having none of it. It wasn't as if she could *force* me. No way.

The girl and I stare at each other while waiting for our luggage and the arrival of the L'Evier car that's supposed to meet us.

"I'm Lucky," I finally say.

She frowns. "I'm not," she says with a bitter twist. "My parents are forcing me to do this."

"Uh . . . I mean my *name* is Lucky," I explain.

She gives me a disgusted look. "That's your *name*?" she says, as if she's never heard anything quite so ridiculous.

She should only know who I'm named after—the notorious gangster Lucky Luciano, whom I guess Gino must've hung with way back in his criminal days.

"Yup," I say. "That's my name. What's yours?"

She hesitates for a moment before revealing that her name is Elizabeth Kate Farrell, only most people call her Liz.

Not a bad name, although no way as cool as Lucky.

The truth is that I *love* my name—it's a one-off, nobody else has it. Besides, if my mom agreed to name me Lucky, then it's all good. It's the "Saint" I'm having a problem with.

"Why are your parents forcing you?" I ask, curious as ever.

"You want the truth or the story I'm supposed to tell?" she says, tugging on her red ponytail.

"Uh, let's go with the truth," I mumble, delighted that someone else might have something to hide.

Liz gives me a long, penetrating look, obviously trying to decide if she can trust me or not.

I stare right back at her, challenging her with my eyes, willing her to go for it.

"Got pregnant. Had an abortion. Now here I am. Banished."

Liz says this all in a very matter-of-fact way. I am totally stunned. Pregnant. An abortion. How old is she anyway?

"Wow," I manage. "That's heavy."

"You think?" she says with a sarcastic grimace.

And then Miss Bossy brings over an elderly emaciated man with pointed features, watery eyes, and a thin mustache. Apparently he is a teacher from L'Evier sent to drive us to the school, located a good hour and a half away from the airport.

The man speaks English with a thick foreign accent. "Come you with me, young ladies," he says, mouth twitching, which causes his whiskery mustache to do a funny little dance. "I am Mr. Lindstrom."

We follow him, trailed by a fat porter who wheels our luggage while breathing heavily, as if near to a major collapse.

By this time I am tired, confused, and filled with questions I wish to ask Liz. If she was pregnant that meant she'd had sex. And if she'd had sex that meant she knew all about it.

As a virgin with absolutely no experience I need to know *everything*.

It's essential.

Details, please.

Everything!

CHAPTER THREE

L'Evier is situated in the middle of nowhere. I am totally shocked. It seems so remote. I can't help getting the feeling that I'm swapping one prison for another. After an endless drive with Mr. Lindstrom at the wheel and Miss Bossy sitting beside him, Liz and I get out of the school car. We glance around the tree-filled courtyard that leads to a tall building covered in ivy. The building looms several stories high, and is not a welcoming sight. Nor is the school principal, who emerges to greet us—well, that's if you can call it a greeting. She is older than the ancient Mr. Lindstrom. She has gray hair worn in a tight bun, exceptionally thin lips, a long nose, and hardly any chin. She wears pebblelike spectacles, a drab brown dress that looks vaguely Amish, and a disapproving expression.

Nice, considering she doesn't even know us yet.

Why do I feel that I'm in the middle of a Charles Dickens novel, transported back in time? Oh sure, I'm an avid reader—that's what you do when you're not allowed out of the house.

Thanks, Daddy Gino.

Did I mention that Gino hates being called "Daddy"? It's Gino all the way, while he calls me "kiddo."

I guess that, on reflection, I have a love-hate relationship with my father. I *want* to love him, but the problem is I always end up hating him for the things he does. Such as the endless women he obviously sleeps with. *Eewh! Disgusting!*

Not that he brings any of them home, but with a house full of staff we always manage to hear about them one way or the other.

As far as I'm concerned, he should've given up women the day my mother was murdered. After all, her murder was *his* fault—it had to be one of his enemies out to get revenge.

Gino does have enemies; Uncle Costa told me that when I'd hotly complained about being confined to what seemed like house arrest. Uncle Costa is not really my uncle. He is Gino's lifelong lawyer and best friend, and Dario and I regard him and his wife, Aunt Jen, as family.

"Your father's a businessman," Costa had informed me. "All businessmen have enemies."

Businessman, huh? I'd researched my father's activities and they encompassed all kinds of business, including— way back—loansharking, running numbers, owning a speakeasy, and, finally, building hotels and casinos in Las

Vegas right at the start of the Vegas boom, turning a patch of barren desert into the shimmering capital of the gambling world.

Yeah. Daddy Dearest has done it all. He's been around and then some.

~ ~ ~

A taxi is outside, ready to take Miss Bossy back to the airport. She can barely throw her uptight ass into it quick enough. "Good-bye, dear," she says, patronizing as ever. "See that you behave yourself."

Then she's gone.

Do I care?

No freaking way!

"Welcome to L'Evier," the woman in the long brown dress says in a most unwelcoming tone. "I am your headmistress. You may refer to me as Miss Miriam." She pauses while her beady eyes behind her pebble spectacles look us over. Her gaze lingers on my T-shirt and her lip curls. Clearly she's not a Rolling Stones fan.

"At L'Evier we keep an extremely strict policy of hard work and complete obedience. You girls are here to learn to become pillars of society, gracious and respectful. A list of rules will be posted in your room, along with your daily uniform. Weekends you may wear your own clothes, however"—another steely look at my T-shirt—"I do expect a certain amount of decorum. No short shorts, torn jeans, or tops worn with no brassiere. L'Evier girls have an image to maintain, so kindly always be sure to uphold our rules or you'll risk immediate expulsion. Remember our motto: 'Girls of Quality—Women of Status.'" A long pause to allow us to absorb her words . . . then, "That will be all for now. Mr. Lindstrom will show you to your quarters."

Quarters? I really have stepped into a Charles Dickens world.

Mr. Lindstrom struggles to retrieve our luggage from the trunk of the old Mercedes he'd driven from the airport. I help him. Liz doesn't. I get the impression she's a bit of a bitch. But I still want to hear everything she has to say about sex.

Does it hurt?

Is it fun?

How do you not get pregnant?

Hmm . . . I guess she'll have no answer to *that* question.

We enter the building, dragging our suitcases behind us since Mr. Lindstrom has now given up. It seems we've been allotted different rooms. Liz is on the first floor, I am on the second. Mr. Lindstrom huffs and puffs all the way to my room, then does a quick vanish.

I fling open the door and there, sitting cross-legged on her bed, is my roommate, a short girl with small blue eyes set in a round face, cascades of the most glorious curly golden hair, very pale skin, and extremely well-developed breasts.

Being more or less flat-chested, I am immediately jealous.

"You must be the new girl," she says, lighting up a cigarette, which I'm sure is not allowed.

"Lucky Saint," I reply, standing awkwardly in the doorway.

"What the hell kind of name is *that*?" she demands, blowing a stream of smoke in my direction.

"And you are?" I say, determined not to let her get to me.

"Olympia Stanislopoulos," she drawls, flicking ash on the carpet. "Welcome to the house of horrors."

Oh my God! This place totally sucks.

CHAPTER FOUR

At first Olympia is not exactly friendly, more wary and inclined to ignore me once she discovers I am a year younger than her. We're in the same grade, which probably pisses her off, because as far as schoolwork goes, I'm smarter, too. I *have* learned something along the way. I speak three languages and I'm a whiz with numbers. I wish I was sharing a room with the infamous Liz. I desperately need some juicy sex education, and she's just the girl to give it to me.

After my fifteenth birthday—celebrated with one candle on a cupcake—and a brief phone call from Daddy Gino, Olympia starts to warm up to me. After all, she's got no choice since we are sleeping in the same room. She tells me about *her* father, Greek shipping billionaire Dimitri Stanislopoulos, divorced from her mom, an American socialite.

"They both like totally spoil the hell outta me," Olympia reveals with an entitled tilt of her head. "It's kinda a one-upmanship deal for them to see who gets the most love. Daddy is desperate for me to marry some rich Greek dude with a ton of money, and Mom figures I should choose a career."

"Doing what?" I ask innocently.

"Beats me," Olympia responds with a casual laugh. "I've been thrown out of two schools, this is the third. Each time they send me farther away."

At least you have both parents, I'm longing to say. But I don't, 'cause I'd learned that once Olympia starts talking, it's best not to interrupt. She's a girl used to getting her own way.

"All *I* wanna do is have fun," Olympia announces. "Boys, booze, and grass. You can join me if you like."

"How's that possible?" I ask. "We're locked up here. Besides, there's nowhere to go."

"Wanna bet?" Olympia says, a big grin lighting up her face. "Lights out at nine-thirty. You 'n' me out the window at nine thirty-five. You on?"

Yes. I am certainly on.

Later that evening we climb out our window, clinging on to the rampant ivy as we skim shakily down a nearby tree.

I feel excited and full of fire. This is the adventure I've been dreaming of.

Once we hit the ground, Olympia grabs a couple of bikes from a covered shed, and we are off.

"Where we going?" I ask, pedaling furiously, while wondering what the punishment will be if we are caught.

"There's a village about twenty minutes away," Olympia says. "We're heading there."

"Really?" I say, slightly wide-eyed, because it's obvious Olympia has done this before.

"Yeah, really," Olympia huffs. "Just follow me and you won't go wrong."

The moment we arrive at the village, Olympia acts very secure—she definitely knows her way around. After parking our bikes, we sit down at an outdoor café, whereupon Olympia orders two coffees laced with a strong liqueur from a waiter who appears to know her. Then she immediately starts flirting with a nearby table full of teenage boys.

Before long several of the boys saunter over to join us. I'm impressed: Olympia certainly knows how to make all the right moves.

None of them speak English. Interesting, because unbeknownst to any of them, I speak fluent German, Italian, and French, so I understand exactly what they're saying. They are all lusting after Olympia, mumbling things like "Fantastic tits!" "I sure hope she screws." "Or sucks." "Or both."

So it's true. Boys only ever want one thing. And since neither of us is about to give it up, I start thinking that we should go. Not that they even notice me. Olympia and her amazing boobs are the main attraction.

"I think we should split," I say at last, starting to feel the effects of the liqueur. I've only been drunk once before, and that was with Dario a couple of Christmases ago. It wasn't a pleasant experience. I prefer being in control, not falling-down drunk.

"No way," Olympia objects. "I'm having fun, aren't you?"

"Actually no," I say. "It's not much fun being ignored, so I'm taking off."

"Nobody's stopping you," Olympia says, completely unconcerned that I'll probably get lost on my way back to the school. What a *bitch*!

Screw it. I grab my bike and hit the road. Like she said—nobody tries to stop me.

I do indeed get lost. And I am mortified when I have to get off my bike, stagger to the side of the road, and throw up. The good news is that I finally make it back to school and crawl under the covers, relieved to not get caught.

Olympia doesn't make it for another three hours. She slips into bed and goes straight to sleep.

When she awakens in the morning she can't wait to tell me what I missed. "Amaze fun," she coos.

"Doing what?" I ask a bit crossly, thinking that maybe I should've stayed.

"Doing almost," Olympia says with a smug smile.

"What's 'almost'?" I ask, still somewhat put out.

"Everything but," Olympia says matter-of-factly.

I still don't get it, until Olympia decides to explain to me in graphic detail the art of "almost."

This turns out to be groping, kissing, playing around, cuddling, fondling, hand jobs, looking. In fact, everything but the final deed.

I finally get it. Oh my God! I have to admit that "almost" does sound like fun, and best of all—no risk of getting pregnant.

After days of instruction, Olympia decides I need to improve the way I look before our next outing. She fusses with my hair, applies my makeup, then lends me a low-cut red sweater, and a very short skirt. Next, she encourages me to stuff my bra with Kleenex until it appears that I have a modicum of cleavage.

I stare in the mirror, no longer a fifteen-year-old girl, more like an eighteen-year-old who looks as if she's been around. I like it!

I wonder what Marco would say if he saw me now.

Ah . . . Marco, I think dreamily. *I love him, I really do.*

"It's time for another walk on the wild side," Olympia announces, applying too much lip gloss with a flourish. "And this time do *not* go racing off like a frightened rabbit."

I don't appreciate her description of my exit. Frightened rabbit indeed! I'm a Santangelo, and Santangelos can do anything they set their mind to.

Equipped with the knowledge that "almost" is the way to go, and clad in Olympia's clothes, we set off, using our usual escape route.

Same café. Same group of boys. Only this time they notice me, and oh yes—I notice them back.

There is one particular boy, Ursi, whom I kind of like. He has long floppy brown hair and kind of a bad-boy look. He wears a leather jacket and speaks a small amount of English.

We start talking. I like his eyes, fringed with thick dark lashes. He likes mine, and I know this because he tells me.

After a while he invites me to go for a walk.

Oh wow! Am I finally going to get that kiss I've been obsessing about?

"Sure," I say, glancing at Olympia for some kind of guidance.

"Go!" she encourages. "We'll catch up later."

Ursi and I set off toward a nearby wooded area. He takes my hand. Exciting. We wander into the woods and after a while he stops, removes his leather jacket, and lays it on the ground.

We sit.

And here it comes . . .

He leans in and kisses me with full probing tongue. Suddenly I realize what all the fuss is about.

Wow! Have I been missing out! Time to start catching up and get myself a real education.

No more little Miss Innocent. I am totally ready to rock 'n' roll!

CHAPTER FIVE

School. What can I tell you? *Boring!* A total waste of time. Stupid cookery classes and sewing and gymnastics—with a few math, Latin, and geography classes thrown in for fun. Did I say fun? Scrub that.

Our math teacher, Miss McGregor, is a witch on wheels. She's around forty with badly dyed black hair and a permanent peevish expression. She hates us all. We hate her back. For some unknown reason she particularly hates me. Maybe it's because I've finally found my voice and I answer back.

She's into giving detention. I am her main target. *Great! Bring it on, witch!*

Sometimes I wonder if I wasn't better off back in Bel Air with no one to talk to except Dario and a series of tutors. Then I realize that as bad as L'Evier is, at least I'm out in the real world making friends and getting kissed.

Ah . . . Ursi. I've seen him a couple of times over the last few weeks, and like Olympia warned me—he's hot to do a lot more than merely kissing.

So far I've managed to stave him off, but right now I'm starting to think what the hell's wrong with "almost"? I can experiment. I *want* to experiment. As long as I keep my cool and don't go all the way, I can certainly try out a few things.

Thank God for Olympia—she's totally awesome and she's already taught me so much. She's like the slightly older sister I never had.

Olympia, Liz, and I have formed an alliance. We're the mavericks in a school full of girls too scared to disobey the rules. Liz has joined us on several of our nighttime excursions. And she's regaled us with stories about the one night she'd had sex and ended up pregnant. We finally got all the gory details. How she was drunk on vodka stolen from her father's study. How the boy—someone she'd only gone out with once before—had insisted that he wasn't going to do anything, he simply wanted to get naked, lie beside her, and gently put it *there* without going any farther.

She was eager to experiment, so—foolish her—she'd believed him.

Naturally he'd slipped her the gold before she'd had the wits to object. And then—weeks later—sixteen and pregnant.

One fast abortion insisted on by her parents, before immediately being shipped off to L'Evier.

I feel for her. She's way cool about it all, but deep down I know she must be hurting.

Olympia thinks it's all a big joke. One thing about Olympia, she takes nothing seriously and who can blame her? Olympia, I discover, has led a privileged life of private planes, Greek islands, New York apartments, and so much luxury. Her father, Dimitri, the billionaire Greek ship owner, is, according to Olympia, a major womanizer.

Hey—join the daddy club, Gino, too.

We have that in common, fathers who can't keep it in their pants.

Liz's dad runs a major movie studio in L.A., while her mom gives great charity lunches every day. According to Liz, neither of them has much time to deal with her, hence the banishment.

Liz's roommate at L'Evier is a beautiful Indian girl called Rashmir. She's very quiet and calm, and would never even think about joining us on our adventures. It's quite obvious that she does not approve of our nocturnal activities, and we can only hope that she doesn't have a fit of "holier than thou" and give us up to the foreboding Miss Miriam. Liz insists she never would, only I'm not so sure.

Hey—whatever. It's my new philosophy. What will be will be, and there's nothing I can do to stop it, so, like Olympia, I'm just going to have fun.

~ ~ ~

Ursi is pleased to see me. He's always pleased to see me, and I'm loving this newfound power I have over the male sex. We meet up in our usual café.

It occurs to me that I have an actual boyfriend, while Olympia and Liz are still playing the field. I feel a bit smug about this, but neither Liz nor Olympia seems the least bit jealous.

After the usual ten minutes of light conversation, Ursi suggests we take a walk.

I'm ready. And willing.

We head for the woods. And this time I'm all set to play.

~ ~ ~

The next morning we're in the science lab working on some useless experiment, when Olympia leans over to me and whispers, "What the hell went on last night? You didn't get back until five A.M."

"I know," I reply with a secretive smile. "You'd better spank me, I'm a *very* bad girl."

Olympia grins. "You catch on fast, don't you? Little Lucky Saint has turned into a total raver. Must be some of me has rubbed off on you."

"You think?"

"Wipe that smug expression off your face and tell me exactly what happened!"

"Almost," I say, unable to stop grinning.

"Did you—?"

"Did I what?"

"Uh . . . did you touch it?"

"Let's just say he's a very happy boy."

"Slut!"

"Takes one to know one."

We exchange knowing smiles.

I have touched a boy. I have felt my power. I am ecstatic.

Now I can't wait to see Marco again. Next time we meet he'll recognize me as the woman I am. Experienced and sophisticated. But still a virgin.

I am saving *that* prize for Marco.

CHAPTER SIX

By the time my first term at L'Evier is over, I am a changed person. I am full of ambition, with dreams of maybe becoming a kickass lawyer or a world-class architect. Both professions appeal to me, although I know nothing about what it would entail to succeed at either of those jobs. It suddenly occurred to me one morning when I woke up that I want to do something powerful. I am woman. I can roar. Getting ready for summer vacation back in L.A., I pack my suitcases and stare at my image in the mirror. So much has happened in three months. I have grown up. I am no longer a fourteen-year-old girl, I am a fifteen-year-old woman. My reflection reveals a different me. With Olympia's encouragement I have cut off my mass of black curly hair, and it's now short and chic. My figure has developed nicely and, oh yeah, I am no longer bare-faced. Makeup is a vast improvement on the natural look.

Ha-ha! Marco is in for a big shock.

Miss Bossy does not come to fetch me. Apparently Miss Bossy got the boot. I couldn't be more delighted.

Liz and I fly together. We are friends. We have plans to do things in L.A. like shopping and dinner, movies and clubbing. Liz assures me she can get me an ace fake ID. Gino cannot stop me now. I'm almost eighteen—give or take three years.

I confide in Liz about my love for Marco.

"How old is he?" she asks, slurping down a bottle of orange juice to which she's added a slug of vodka. Liz loves her booze—she buys it from a girl at school whose mom works for an airline and comes home loaded with miniatures, which her daughter promptly steals and sells.

"Dunno," I answer vaguely. "Twenty-eight maybe. Or thirty."

Liz wrinkles her nose. "That's old."

"I don't care," I answer recklessly. "I love him."

"Do you think he likes you back?" Liz inquires.

I wish.

I shrug.

I eventually fall asleep.

~ ~ ~

Oh yes, dreams do come true. Marco is at the airport, waiting to meet me.

I stare at him.

He stares right through me.

Oh my God! He doesn't even recognize me.

And then he does, because I run over, tap him on the arm, and say, "Remember me?"

"Lucky?" he asks, as if he can't quite believe it's me.

"You got it in one," I reply, excited to see him.

"Jesus!" he exclaims, and not in an admiring way. "What'd you do to your hair?"

I give him a sexy look. "How do you like the new me?" I ask, waiting for an enthusiastic response.

"Uh . . . it's certainly different," he says, signaling a porter to take my luggage.

"Well . . . uh . . . *I'm* certainly different," I say boldly. "You can call me a woman of experience." I throw him a jaunty wink. "Know what I mean?"

Marco starts to choke. Not the reaction I'd expected.

"Let's go," he says at last, his voice gruff. "And you better wash some of that clown makeup off before Gino sees you, otherwise you'll be dead meat."

I'm outraged. *Screw you, Marco.* Is that all you've got to say to me?

I hate him. I really do.

~ ~ ~

"You look gruesome!" Dario shrieks the moment I enter the house.

"Thanks a lot," I reply, furious because he obviously

doesn't get it, just like Marco, who didn't say a word to me on the drive from the airport.

I am royally pissed and upset and disappointed. What is wrong with these creeps? Can't they see I'm all grown up?

Dario trails me up to my bedroom, desperately trying to make amends for his stupid comment.

"I guess I'll get used to you looking like one of those girls from Aunt Jen's fashion mags," he says. "It's not so bad."

A reluctant compliment if ever I heard one.

I decide to forgive him—after all, he is my brother and I have missed him. Sort of.

"Where's Gino?" I ask.

"Vegas," Dario says, plunking himself down on my bed.

"Nice of him to be here to welcome me home," I complain, reaching for the pack of cigarettes I have stashed in my purse.

"When did you start smoking?" Dario inquires, obviously impressed.

"At school," I reply, adding a mysterious "I learned a lot of things at school."

Dario nods approvingly while I light up and offer him a drag. He eagerly accepts. We exchange smiles. I finally decide it's good to be home with my little brother.

"Dad's got himself a new girlfriend," Dario reveals. "And she's famous."

I am still wondering why Marco hasn't fallen at my feet

and declared his undying love for me; however, Dario's statement jolts me back to reality.

"Famous?" I question, frowning. "Who is she?"

"A movie star," Dario says.

Could he be more vague?

"No shit," I say irritably. "Does she have a name?"

"Marabelle Blue."

I slowly digest this piece of unbelievable information. Marabelle Blue is a huge freaking star, kind of a major sex symbol. What the f—?

"You're kidding," I finally manage.

"It's true," Dario assures me.

"How do you know?" I press, eager for more information.

"He brings her here," Dario says, savoring the moment. "I've seen them screwing."

I almost choke on my cigarette. Actually, I'm not that into smoking, but hey, I'm well aware that it makes me look way cool.

"You haven't," I say, all kinds of images floating before my eyes.

"Oh yes I have," Dario crows. "Watched 'em through the bedroom keyhole."

"You sneaky little rat," I exclaim.

Dario throws his blond head back and laughs. "It was major."

"I bet."

"And get this," Dario adds.

"What?" I ask with a fed-up sigh.

"Gino's flying back from Vegas and bringing her here for dinner tonight."

"No way," I say, totally alarmed.

"Way," Dario says, confirming the bad news.

I realize I'd better get myself together if we're having dinner with a movie star.

Will I like her?

Who cares? She won't be around long enough for it to matter.

CHAPTER SEVEN

What is it with the male members of my so-called family? First Marco, then Dario, now Gino himself, all carrying on about how they hate my hair and makeup and clothes. What? Did they expect me to stay looking like a lanky teen-ager forever? I have moved on, thank you very much, and I don't care what any of them have to say. Well, that's not absolutely true, because I do care about Marco—not that he's family, thank God, because if he *was* family, I couldn't end up marrying him, and quite obviously that's what's going to happen. Eventually.

Is Daddy Dearest pleased to see me?

I don't know. I can't tell. He seems distant.

When I was younger—before my mom's murder—he used to call me his little Italian princess, throw me in the air, and smother me with hugs and kisses.

Now all I get is criticism.

I don't care.

Yes I do.
No. I don't.

~ ~ ~

Marabelle Blue turns out to be a larger-than-life dreamy creature with big blue eyes, flowing platinum blonde hair, quivering red jammy lips, and huge breasts. She wears a pink chiffon dress cut down to Cuba, and sparkly diamond earrings that seem as if they might be the real thing. She looks as if she should be going to a movie premiere, not dinner at our house.

"Hi, Lucky," she murmurs in a breathy, little-girl voice. "Your daddy's told me all about you—it's such a pleasure to finally meet you."

Is it? Why?

I mumble a suitable greeting and throw Gino a killer glare. Is this to be my welcome-home celebration? Dinner with a big-deal movie star whom I automatically hate because she's sleeping with my father?

I flash onto Ursi, thinking about the things I did with him, and wondering if Marabelle Fishface does the same things with Gino.

I shudder at the thought. Unthinkable!

"Y'know," Gino says, giving me one of his major annoying looks, "Marabelle could take you to the studio, show you around an' get you some makeup lessons so's you don't look like such a clown."

My eyes fill with tears. A clown? Is he freaking *kidding* me? What is it with him and Marco? Why do they both say the same things?

"I'd be happy to," Marabelle says, aiming to please. "Anytime you like, sweetie."

I refuse to let them see me cry. Holding back my tears, I pick up a glass of water and pretend to semi-choke.

"An' you should grow your hair back," Gino growls. "Ya look like a goddamn boy."

Ah, yes. Another fantastic dinner with my loving and sensitive father.

After the dinner ordeal is over I race up to my room, lock the door, and sob it out. I'm entitled. I only have one parent.

Where's Mommy when I need her? Why did she have to go and get herself murdered? It isn't fair. It's all Gino's fault. And what has he done about it?

Exactly nothing. Shouldn't he be out tracking her killer? Not sleeping with vacuous movie stars.

Dario hammers on my door. I yell at him to go away. He keeps hammering. I shout at him to screw off.

I phone Liz. She isn't home.

I wander into my bathroom and gaze intently at my re-flection, leaning close to the mirror to get a better look. A river of tears has obliterated my carefully applied eye makeup. Gino's right—now I look like a *sad* clown.

Unfortunate fact. I *am* a sad clown.

I was so happy about coming home and impressing

everyone. Unfortunately, things haven't played out the way I'd planned in my head, and I don't know who to blame except myself.

But *is* it my fault?

No. It's Gino's and his raging libido. *I hate him. I love him. I hate him. I love him.* Same old story.

In the morning I call Olympia in Greece.

"Miss you," she says.

Her words put a smile on my face. "You, too," I respond.

"How is it there?" she asks.

"Horrible," I reply. "Gino's hooked up with some dumb movie star, and everyone's being mean to me."

"A movie star?" Olympia questions, far more interested in my movie star comment than the fact that everything else sucks. "What's her name?"

"Marabelle Blue."

"Holy knockers," Olympia exclaims in awe. "Marabelle Blue is huge!"

"Huge knockers you mean," I say with a wayward giggle. "She was at our house for dinner last night and they were like falling out of her dress. So gross!"

Olympia roars with laughter. "Good job *my* dad wasn't there," she says. "He's such a letch, he'd have been all over that in a second."

"I was thinking . . ." I say, thoughts forming.

"Like what are you thinking?"

"Well . . . I'm kind of desperate," I venture. "Is there any chance I can come stay with you for the summer?"

"Now, that's a *fantastic* idea!" Olympia squeals, sounding genuinely delighted. "You are *so* invited. We can have ourselves an incredible time."

"Of course, I'll have to get permission from Gino," I say, warming to the idea. "That should be easy, though, 'cause he's so preoccupied with Marabelle Fishface that I'm sure he'll say yes."

"Yippee! Can't wait," Olympia says, full of enthusiasm. "You gotta bring your sexiest bikinis—'cause it's all sun, sea, and sand here. You'll *love* it. *And* you can get an amazing tan."

"Are you sure it'll be okay with your family?"

"No prob."

I wait for the right moment to ask Gino if I can go. He is on his way to his hotel in Vegas and seems quite preoccupied. "Who are these people you want to stay with?" he asks.

"It's my best friend, Olympia Stanislopoulos," I inform him. "Her parents have a big villa on an island in Greece. They have their own yacht and plenty of security in residence—just like us, so it's perfectly safe."

I fail to mention that Olympia's parents are divorced and that Mrs. Stanislopoulos will not be around.

Gino nods. Exactly as I thought, he has Marabelle Fishface on his mind, and I'm sure he doesn't want me hanging about getting in his way.

"Yeah," he grunts. "I guess if that's what you've made up your mind t'do. Call my secretary, have her make the

arrangements an' give her all the details 'bout where you'll
be an' who'll be watchin' out for you. Oh, yeah . . . an'
Lucky—"

"Yes, Gino?"

"Make sure you behave yourself," he adds, giving me
a hard look. "No drinking. No boys. No screwin' around.
Got it?"

"Of course, Gino," I say, obedient daughter to the hilt.

Oh! He should only know the things that I have already
done. And the truth is I don't regret one single minute of
any of them!

CHAPTER EIGHT

Before I leave for the Greek islands, Liz and I spend a day together. Liz drives her dad's Porsche. He's in New York and her mom's at a spa, so there is no one to stop her. Naturally she drives too fast; I don't care, it's kind of exciting. We hit Melrose, Robertson, and Third Street. We have lunch on the beach in Venice. We buy tops and jeans and shoes and all kinds of delicious stuff. We cruise the boardwalk and get into flirty conversations with random boys. Later we go back to her house in the Palisades, where we sit around smoking and trying on our new outfits.

Liz raids her dad's study and reappears with a full bottle of vodka. She really does like her booze. Me, not so much. Getting wasted strikes me as rather stupid. I kind of like having a clear picture of what's going on.

After a while Liz decides to invite a bunch of friends over. Before long it turns into a party.

Somehow or other I find myself on a couch with a tattooed guy called Brad, and before long it's "almost" time.

Hmm . . . I am getting pretty sure of myself, but after a while Brad—who must be at least nineteen—wants more, and he's becoming quite aggressive about it.

I manage to extract myself and go find Liz, who is now totally wasted. The girl shouldn't drink—doesn't she remember what happened to her last time?

I realize there's no way she can leave her own party to take me home even if she is capable of driving—which she's not, so I call a cab, although I feel a bit guilty about leaving Liz without a friend by her side, 'cause all the other girls seem to have paired off with guys. A lot of "almost" is taking place, and more besides.

This party is fast turning into a free-for-all and I want out. Besides, it's verging on midnight and I have an eleven o'clock curfew. Not that it matters—Gino's in Vegas. Apparently he couldn't care less.

Liz is out of it by the pool, passed out on a lounger. I think that maybe she'll sleep it off.

My cabdriver doesn't speak a word of English; he drives along Sunset as if he's in a to-the-death race. As soon as we hit Bel Air he gets lost, then when he finds our house, he gouges me on the fare.

Reluctantly I pay up, head up the stone stairs, throw open the front door, and there is Marco, standing in the front hall, furious.

"You know the rules," he scolds, steaming and oh-so-handsome. "Home by eleven, an' never—*I repeat, never*—put your dumb ass in an L.A. cab. They're friggin' death traps."

I throw him a haughty look. "You're not Gino," I mutter. "You can't tell me what to do."

This infuriates him even more. "You got yourself one helluva smart mouth in Switzerland, huh?" he says, scowling, which only makes him look even *more* handsome.

"That's not all I got," I reply, hotfooting it up to the safety of my room before he can say anything more.

What am I supposed to do about Marco? It's so obvious he has feelings for me. How come he can't relax and admit it?

I smile to myself. Is he jealous that I'm out and about? Is he wondering what I am doing and with whom?

Too bad, Marco—you had your opportunity and you blew it.

~ ~ ~

The next morning I am up early, packed, and ready to go. Dario is skulking around with a pissed-off expression. I'd made a promise to spend the summer with him, only things have changed. Besides, Dario is still a kid. What would we do together? Play Scrabble and stare at the TV all day? I think not.

Olympia is waiting, and I'm on my way.

Marco drives me to the airport in stony silence.

I have so many questions I want to ask him, but I sense that now is not the time.

Do you have a girlfriend?

Do you want a girlfriend?

What do you really think of me?

And the biggest question of all—*when will you finally acknowledge that we belong together?*

I step out of the car at the airport. There is a VIP escort waiting to take me to the plane. Marco takes my luggage from the trunk, hands it over to a porter, gets back in the car, and drives off without so much as a good-bye.

Screw you, Marco! I scream in my head. *I hate you, too!*

~ ~ ~

On the plane I am seated next to an obese man with bad breath and an urge to flirt.

Ugh! He is major old and quite disgusting. I yearn for the voluptuous bimbo I was seated next to on my first trip to Europe.

The flight attendant walks down the aisle offering newspapers. I grab an *LA Times* and bury my nose in it. Maybe the old dude will take a hint and stop trying to hit on me.

I am not really reading the newspaper, merely trying to

appear occupied, when the headline of a story catches my eye.

TEENAGE DAUGHTER OF STUDIO MOGUL DROWNS IN FAMILY POOL

For a second my heart stops. It can't be . . . can it?

I am too nervous to read on. But then I do, and the story is all there in black and white.

Elizabeth Farrell, daughter of studio head Martin B. Farrell and philanthropist Lindsay Farrell, was discovered drowned in the family swimming pool by a caretaker at three o'clock this morning.

I choke back a scream. My eyes fill with tears.

I shouldn't have left her. It's all my fault.

I slump down in my seat and do not utter a word until the plane lands, whereupon I spy Olympia in the waiting area and fall into her arms, sobbing my heart out.

~ ~ ~

For the next few days we mourn together. Olympia is a true friend. She keeps on assuring me that it had nothing to do with me, that I wasn't Liz's keeper, and that what happened to her was a freak accident.

I am not convinced, but what the hell, I have to learn to move on. I moved on after my mom's death even though I was just a child. I clearly remember Gino's words: "Don't ever forget you're a Santangelo. Never let 'em see you crumble."

Yes. I am a Santangelo, more like Gino than I care to admit.

Gradually I put what happened to Liz out of my mind and begin to enjoy the summer.

CHAPTER NINE

The Stanislopoulos villa, located on its own private island, is spectacular. It's perched on a bluff overlooking the azure-blue Mediterranean, and there are endless terraces and incredible views. The Stanislopoulos luxury yacht rests in the bay. Olympia's dad, Dimitri, is an imposing man with a deep suntan, craggy features, and a prominent nose. Handsome, I suppose, in an older-man kind of way. He greets me with a kiss on each cheek, then a third one for good luck, followed by an all-enveloping hug. He smells of very expensive aftershave, cigars, and strong liquor.

"Welcome, my dear," he says in a loud booming voice. "Any friend of my Olympia's will fit right in here. We are all one big happy family."

After that he more or less ignores me, which is okay because Villa Stanislopoulos is teeming with people. Relatives and houseguests, attractive older women in designer beachwear, and a bunch of noisy kids. Apart from a sour-faced French girl, we are the only teenagers.

"Who are all these people?" I ask. "They seem to change daily."

"I know," Olympia agrees, with a nod of her blonde head. "All you gotta do is smile while attempting to avoid the old letches. They'll try to grab your ass given half a chance, so move quickly. They're ancient and not so nimble."

She was right. The older the man, the more his hands seemed to be about to wander.

Gross! Ancient Greeks in mankinis exhibiting protruding bellies and pathetic packages while lying out by the infinity pool to further their leathered suntans.

This is not the vacation I had hoped for.

"Isn't there anywhere else we can go?" I ask restlessly after a couple of days. "Y'know, like take off for the day? Explore somewhere different?"

Olympia gets the hint. "I was waiting for you to give me the word," she says. "After what happened to Liz and all . . ." she trails off.

"I'm about ready for some fun," I say, determined not to feel guilty about Liz forever. Unfortunately, Liz chose the path she wished to take, and as much as I'll miss her, it's time to move on. I refuse to keep blaming myself. Besides, I know how Gino would act, and sometimes I'm more like my father than I think.

"Not to worry," Olympia replies with a jaunty wink. "I'm plotting our next move right now!"

~ ~ ~

Our next move suits me just fine. A Riva motorboat trip from the island to the mainland—a popular vacation resort teeming with tourists and boys, boys, boys!

We're supposed to stick with one of Olympia's aunts who has accompanied us, but that's not the way it's going down.

Aunt Alethea is a blonde languid woman who seems more interested in perusing the shops than spending time with us. She graciously hands us money, tells us to go enjoy ourselves, and reminds us to meet her at the dock at 6:30 P.M. ready to return to our island.

"Your aunt is way cool!" I say with enthusiasm.

"That's 'cause she has a boyfriend she secretly meets up with," Olympia reveals with a knowing smirk. "It's all very under the radar—he's black, and she doesn't want anyone to know."

"Then how *do* you know?" I ask, quite impressed with this nugget of private info.

Olympia gives a mysterious smile. "I have ways of finding out everything, so . . . if you're hiding anything . . ."

I immediately flash onto Gino telling me that my name is Lucky Saint, and not to mention my true identity to anyone. "It's for your own safety, kiddo," he'd assured me. "Listen to what I say. Got it?"

As usual, I got it.

Now I wonder if Olympia knows who I really am? Lucky Santangelo, daughter of the infamous Gino. The girl whose mother was murdered, and whose father is notorious.

And if she doesn't, should I tell her? She's my first close friend and it might be a relief to be truthful.

I decide against it. Who knows how she'll react.

We hit a crowded beach and mingle. No security. No watchful eyes. Simply two girls out to have a fine old time. Olympia is way into it; so am I. We pay for a couple of loungers, strip off our coverups, and lie out in our bikinis. Olympia all blonde and curvaceous, me so dark and lean. We make an inviting couple.

Although they are not in Olympia's class, I now have boobs—hardly huge—but in my eyes just right.

Before long a boy—accidentally or on purpose—trips over the end of Olympia's lounger. Mister Cool he's not, although he is kind of interesting looking with long flaxen hair and a crooked smile.

"Sorry," he says in accented English.

Olympia throws him an appraising look and deems him acceptable to flirt with. "Okay," she says. "What's going on in this place? Anything exciting we should know about?"

"Tourists?" he asks.

"From L.A.," I say.

"I can show you around," he offers, quickly latching on to what he sees as two hot babes out to have an adventure.

Olympia, who is fluent in both Greek and English, decides that she is also from L.A. and speaks only English. Olympia gets off on screwing with her would-be conquests.

He happily buys it.

"You play the table tennis?" he asks.

We both nod, although I know for a fact that Olympia has never played in her life. I happen to be a champion, having indulged in nothing but endless games with Dario for what seems like years.

"You come play with me and my friends," he says, proffering his hand to Olympia.

"Okay," Olympia says, allowing him to pull her up. "You got a name?"

"Borus," he says.

"I'm Olympia," she says. "And this is Lucky."

I can see she's kind of into him, and since he tripped over Olympia first, I guess I'm supposed to back off. She has dibs.

I only hope he has some cute friends, 'cause I'm in the mood to play, and I don't mean Ping-Pong. "Almost" has become my favorite game.

Borus's friends turn out to be a mixed group, with girls outnumbering boys, which I find quite disappointing.

They are all gathered at the top of the beach where there are several Ping-Pong tables set out. It seems that they are in the middle of a tournament.

Borus has totally zeroed in on Olympia and I'm starting

to get that left-out feeling. Now that I have experienced my power over boys, I'm hungry for more.

I check out the group. There is one boy who instantly attracts my attention. The problem is that he appears to be with a girl.

Shame.

Or is it?

It's not as if they're married or anything. He probably just picked her up on the beach like Borus did with Olympia.

I go for a move, full of confidence I never realized I had. Striding over, I say, "Hi. I'm Lucky." I say it to both the girl and the guy so that she doesn't get all pissy on me.

"Wassup?" he mumbles, looking me over with a moody expression.

"Are you American?" I ask.

"'S right," he replies, brushing back a lock of dark hair that's practically falling into his eyes. Dark eyes, too, just my type.

The girl throws me a dirty look. She has short brown hair and wears a not-very-flattering polka-dot bikini.

"Hi." I repeat my greeting to her.

She pulls on Mister Dark Eyes's arm and attempts to drag him away.

He's not having it; he shakes free and grins at me. "Lulu doesn't speak English," he says. "She's French."

"Then how do you communicate?" I ask.

He winks at me in a very knowing way. "How d'you think?"

"I think you should dump her and come play Ping-Pong with me," I suggest.

Bold! Even I am startled by the words coming out of my mouth.

"You do, huh?" says Mister Dark Eyes.

I can tell he likes my attitude. "Oh yeah," I assure him. "I promise you will not regret it."

And that is how my big vacation hookup started.

CHAPTER TEN

His name is Brandon. He's eighteen and he's from Queens, New York. He's visiting Greece on vacation with his parents, and he's major sexy. I inform him that I am seventeen, soon to be eighteen myself.

Naturally he believes me. I have turned into a totally smooth and convincing liar—especially when it comes to fudging my age. After all, if he realizes I'm only fifteen—game over.

After I show off my prowess at Ping-Pong with Brandon as my partner, Lulu glares at me and runs off in a tearful huff. Not my fault.

Olympia and Borus and Brandon and I buy time on a couple of pedal boats and take to the sea, whereupon pedaling becomes secondary to full-on kissing.

Brandon is a great kisser, better than Ursi.

I like it! I like it! Why have I waited so long?

After a while Brandon informs me that he has to have

dinner with his parents but that we should get together later on the beach. Sounds like a plan to me.

Once we hit land, I confer with Olympia, who I discover is equally eager to spend more time with Borus.

Question: How do we deal with Aunt Alethea and our 6:30 P.M. rendezvous to return to the Stanislopoulos island?

Olympia immediately comes up with a plan. That's what I love about Olympia—she's always thinking ahead.

"Our story is that you ran into a cousin you haven't seen in ages," she announces. "Which means we have to stay for dinner, and they should send the Riva back for us at eleven."

"Great," I say. "D'you think your dad'll buy it?"

"Course he will, he's so busy with his guests," Olympia says, tossing back her long blonde curls. "There's no way he'll even notice we're missing."

It occurs to me that Gino and Dimitri are very similar types of men. Handsome macho dudes who care only about themselves. It's no wonder Olympia and I have forged such a close friendship—we're sisters from another life.

"What'll we wear?" I ask, realizing that all we've got are the bikinis we're standing up in, plus flimsy coverups.

"No prob," Olympia says, groping in her purse and producing an AmEx card. "While the boys have dinner with their families, the girls'll go shopping! Right?"

I'm so glad I have a friend like Olympia; she's on it all the way.

~ ~ ~

Later we meet up with Aunt Alethea at the dock. Olympia's aunt looks flushed and slightly dreamy-eyed. She's forty-something. Do people of that advanced age still enjoy sex?

Apparently so, for it's written all over her face that she was doing a lot more than shopping—even though she's armed with several shopping bags.

Olympia feeds her our story and of course she buys it. We skip away from the dock, triumphant. I have to say that I'm loving every second of this adventure. I'm happier than I've ever been. I am finally living my life, and surely it's about time!

We shop outrageously. Olympia informs me that her dad never checks her credit card bills, they simply get paid by an anonymous accountant who questions nothing.

I don't even *have* a credit card. Gino's into keeping me under strict control.

Yeah. Right. That's yesterday's news. I am no longer Daddy's little puppet. I am a free agent, free as the breeze! And nobody can stop me now, not even Gino.

After our shopping spree, we retire to an open-air café in a busy square. I am now wearing my new outfit of tight white jeans and a cropped red tank. Dead sexy. Brandon's gonna love it. Olympia is in a short pink dress that shows off her amazing boobs to full advantage, nipples front and center. All new purchases courtesy of Olympia's credit card.

I have to say that we both look major hot.

I can't wait to meet up with Brandon again—I'm already fantasizing about how far I'll let him go. Not all the way, of course, but with "almost" there are several inventive ways to play the game without risking getting pregnant.

Olympia sips a coffee laced with her favorite liqueur. I stick to a cappuccino and a baguette sandwich—which is good considering I'm now starving. Olympia is not; she only eats when she feels like it.

Borus turns up at exactly nine, the designated time of meeting. He's wearing linen shorts, a striped shirt, and flip-flops. Hardly Mister Sex on a Stick. I imagine Brandon will look way cooler. I can hardly wait!

Borus is friendly, but I can tell he is impatient to get Olympia to himself.

I consult my watch. Brandon is late. We'd arranged to meet at nine o'clock and it is now almost nine-thirty.

Olympia doesn't want to leave me sitting in the café alone, which is thoughtful of her, but I insist that she and Borus take off.

Borus doesn't need to hear me say it twice. He grabs Olympia's arm and pulls her up. She giggles and gives me a look as if to say "What can I do?"

"Go!" I encourage. "See you on the dock at eleven."

It seems a bit weird sitting by myself, especially when two older creeps camped out at a nearby table start checking me out. Ugh! Old men with fat bellies and lecherous eyes. I bet they're married, too.

By ten I decide that I can't sit there anymore looking like a total loser. Maybe if I get up and take a walk, Brandon will miraculously appear. It's obvious his stupid parents are holding him up—I guess that's the kind of thing parents do. Like I wouldn't know.

I wander down toward the sea, and as I approach I suddenly see them! Brandon and Lulu are standing by the entrance to the beach, locking lips like there's no tomorrow.

Oh . . . my . . . God!

For a moment I am frozen in time—a pathetic little teenager struck in the face by the reality of it all. I want to either burst into tears or seriously throw up.

Suddenly I am filled with a surge of fury, and I make up my mind to do neither. Screw it! I'm a Santangelo, not stupid little Lucky Saint.

I purposefully walk by them, making sure that they see me, even though it's kind of dark. "Hey, Brandon," I say—cool and casual as if I really couldn't give a rat's ass.

Brandon unlocks lips and throws me a look. "Wassup?" he mutters, while Lulu gives off a triumphant sneer.

I shrug. "Gotta go," I say, winking. Yes, I actually do a cringe-worthy wink! "Hot date waiting. Y'know how it is."

"Hey—" he starts to say.

Before he can finish, I'm gone—walking away as quickly as possible.

Boys.
Not to be trusted.
Not to be believed.
I'm getting the message.

CHAPTER ELEVEN

Olympia is not as sympathetic as I expected. She arrives at the dock ten minutes late with messed-up hair, smeared lipstick, and a burgeoning hickey on her neck. Lovely. I get dumped and she gets to make out. I'm jealous.

I relay my sad story. Olympia gives a casual shrug. "Boys are dicks," she announces. "Thing is there's so many of them around that it doesn't really matter. They're like trains—one rolls out, another rolls in. Don't sweat it."

Sometimes Olympia is smarter than she looks.

We make it back to our private island where Olympia's dad is having some kind of Greek dance-off with multiple friends and relatives. The music is loud. The natives are drunk. It's all too much.

"Bed," Olympia whispers. "Don't even think about joining in."

As if I was. No way. Old people letting loose has never been my thing.

I sleep fitfully, thinking about dumbass Brandon. Was it something I did? Said? Where did I go wrong?

Finally I decide that it isn't me, it's *him*. *He's* the asshole. I'm a Santangelo, and I refuse to be disrespected by some lame boy.

~ ~ ~

The next morning I am all revved up and hot for revenge. "Can we go back to town?" I beg Olympia, who is looking very sleepy-eyed and pleased with herself.

"Not today," she says with a casual wave of her hand. "Poppa wants us on the yacht."

"Why?" I ask, frowning.

Olympia giggles. "Set decoration for all the old farts to ogle."

I am not thrilled with this plan. I need to spit in Brandon's face—not literally, but somehow I have a strong urge to get back at him.

"Tomorrow," Olympia promises, sensing my disappointment. "Today we'll work on getting the best tan *ever*."

"Okay," I say, still seething about Brandon.

The Stanislopoulos yacht is quite amazing. The crew even more so. Why hasn't Olympia mentioned that her father's yacht is teeming with a crew of supersexy young guys in tight white uniforms?

"Wow!" I give her a delighted nudge. "These guys rock!"

"Hands and eyes off," Olympia warns. "They work for Poppa. Forbidden territory."

Forbidden, my ass, I think. They might be forbidden to her, but hey—I'm a visitor, I can do what I want.

There is one particular member of the crew who immediately grabs my attention. His name is Jack and I soon find out he's an Australian. I spend the day trying to stir up some kind of conversation without Olympia noticing. It isn't easy, but I think I manage to get through to him.

Before we leave the yacht I ask him if he ever goes into town.

This obviously takes him by surprise, but I can tell he's interested.

"Yeah, sometimes," he says, glancing around to make sure he's not being watched by one of his superiors.

"Tomorrow?" I question. "We could meet up."

"We could," he says unsurely. "It's my day off. So . . ."

"See you by the main beach at noon," I say, adding a quick "And in case you're wondering, I'm eighteen, so I'm totally legal."

He looks relieved, but still wary. Fraternizing with the guests is obviously a big no-no.

I smile to myself. Flirting is so easy, and yet majorly empowering. Men. Boys. Old farts. They're all the same. A provocative smile, a flash of suntanned skin, a toss of dark hair. It's all a game, and I am fast learning how to be a power player.

~ ~ ~

Fortunately, Olympia is itching to meet up with Borus again. "What'll *you* do if I go off with Borus all day?" she asks as we board the Riva for another day trip to the mainland. "There's no way I'm leaving you by yourself."

"Don't worry about me," I say with a casual shrug. "I like lying out on the beach by myself. It's relaxing, and I can keep an eye out for any interesting prospects."

"Whatever," Olympia says, adding a not-very-enthusiastic "It's okay if you tag along with us."

"No thanks," I say, thinking that Jack better turn up or else.

I have a plan. It'll work, I know it will. I vaguely recall listening in one day when Gino was talking to Uncle Costa. "You always gotta have a plan, an' you always gotta stick to it." Those were Gino's words of wisdom.

Yes, Daddy Gino, I think I am taking your advice.

Shortly before noon I linger at the top of the beach near the Ping-Pong tables. I have borrowed a red bikini from Olympia and cleverly stuffed the bra cups with socks for extra appeal.

Looking sexy works, and big boobs are obviously sexy.

Apparently so, for who comes trotting up but Brandon, alone and primed for action.

"Wassup?" he mutters.

A boy of few words.

"Not much," I reply, licking my lips in a vaguely suggestive way. "You?"

"Thought I'd take a ride on one of those pedalos," he mumbles. "Wanna come?"

"Don't think so," I reply, cool and in control.

His face registers shock. It's obvious Brandon—with his brooding good looks—is not used to getting turn-downs. "Why not?" he demands.

"'Cause I'm busy," I say, keeping it casual.

"You don't look busy t'me," Brandon says, squinting at me.

"I will be."

He cocks an eyebrow. "You pissed about the other day?"

"Are you kidding?" I retort.

"It was nothin'," Brandon continues. "She's a hanger-on. I was just trying to get her off my back."

"Or front," I murmur.

"You *are* pissed," he says triumphantly.

"I am so not," I reply.

And then—thank you, God—up strolls Jack in white shorts and a black T-shirt. Tall and tan, an all-Australian hunk.

Without thinking it through, I throw my arms around Jack's neck and plant a kiss firmly on his lips.

He is shocked but game.

Brandon is livid.

"This is my boyfriend," I say to Brandon.

"Hey," Brandon says, simmering.

Jack gets what's going on and plays along.

"Hello, mate," he says. "Thanks for keepin' an eye on my girl." And with that he grips my arm and whisks me away.

As soon as we are out of earshot Jack starts to laugh. "You're a cheeky little minx," he guffaws. "What're you up to?"

"The dude deserved it," I reply. "He played me, so I played him back."

"And you used me."

"I know," I say, stopping for a moment and giving him a long lingering look. "And for that I owe you. So . . . how would you like me to repay you?"

We spent the rest of the day on the beach making out under a large sun umbrella. I soon realize I have picked well; Jack is an amazing kisser, even better than Brandon—who was not lacking in the kissing department.

I am becoming a woman of experience and I like it!

It occurs to me that the male species is easy to manipulate as long as you know how to play it. And, believe me, I am learning fast!

CHAPTER TWELVE

After an amazing summer in Greece, it's back to the same old—and by that I mean L'Evier and unbelievably tedious lessons on subjects I have absolutely no interest in. Latin, anyone? Geometry? And of course there are even more boring rules—which Olympia and I have no problem breaking. Since we both get off on taking risks, our night-time outings are becoming more and more frequent. All I can say is thank God for Olympia, she's my partner in everything—and although at the beginning of our friendship she taught *me* a thing or two, I have now caught up big-time. Oh yes. I might only be fifteen, but I've certainly learned how to deal with boys. No more stupid schoolgirl crushes—I have developed a "don't call me, I'll call you" mentality. I give 'em "almost"—which drives them insane—and I stay in control. It's the only way.

Shortly after getting back to school I see on TV that Marabelle Blue has gotten engaged to a businessman by the name of Gino Santangelo. Businessman indeed! What a crock! Thank God I'm not connected to him. Nobody knows who I really am.

Ms. Blue's engagement takes place six weeks after her very public suicide attempt. Great. Am I about to welcome a psycho suicide freak as my stepmom?

Ugh!

Daddy Dearest phones to tell me of his engagement.

Too late, Gino, I saw it on the news. Thanks for your concern.

I can't help wondering how Dario feels. I *do* miss him, although he's still a little kid, and I'm all grown up. We probably don't have much in common anymore.

Tonight Olympia and I take a major risk. We sneak out, get totally wasted, and smuggle two boys back to our school and into our room. Talk about daring!

My date for the night's activities, Chad, has brown curly hair and a very nice bod. He is English and attends the boys' school located near us. I am quite taken with his accent, and his kissing skills aren't bad either.

I've never actually practiced "almost" in a bed before. But soon I am totally naked with a boy for the first time. Naturally this horny English boy is hot to take it all the way.

"Everything but," I tell him firmly, wriggling out of his reach.

"C'mon," he begs. "Let me just put it there, between your legs—I promise I won't do anything."

Ah yes, and I have a fine piece of real estate in Central Park I can sell you . . .

Boys! They must think all girls are total idiots.

I dissuade him from his task by doing something to him that all boys crave. Then just when he is about to return the favor, the lights go on, and standing in the doorway to our room—arms crossed, looking like a stern-faced ghost—is the gym teacher, and Miss Miriam herself.

Holy batshit!

Crapola major!

Man!

"Out!" Miss Miriam thunders at the two boys, who leap from our beds as if they have raging frogs up their asses. "Go now. And never return."

The boys frantically grab their clothes and run, leaving me and Olympia hiding under the sheets in our individual beds.

"Tomorrow morning. My office," Miss Miriam says, laser eyes decimating us. Then she snaps off the lights with an ominous flourish and the two women make a stern exit.

Olympia dissolves into fits of nervous giggles.

I don't know what to do. So I laugh, too.

Screw it. We're invincible!

~ ~ ~

"You have brought disgrace upon the entire establishment of L'Evier. This hallowed school has *never* experienced behavior like this before. *Never!*" Miss Miriam removes her pebblelike spectacles and glares at us.

For a moment I think she might burst into tears at the effrontery of it all. But she doesn't—she curls her lip and continues glaring.

It's the next morning and we are standing in her office in front of her desk like a couple of criminals caught in the act. I guess in her eyes that's exactly what we are.

Miss Miriam is on a rant. "To bring boys into my school is bad enough. But to take them to your room, and to be found *in bed* with them. Well . . ."

Olympia stifles a giggle.

Miss Miriam turns on her. "You may well laugh, young lady—however, I do not imagine your laughter will continue when your father arrives to remove you from this school that you have besmirched with your *disgusting* vulgar behavior."

Olympia gulps. So do I.

"The pair of you are expelled," Miss Miriam continues. "Both your fathers will be here tomorrow morning to collect you. In the meantime you are to go to your room and *stay* there. Is that clear?"

We nod, only now I'm panicking. Has the old biddy contacted Gino? Will he be coming for me? Jeez, I am in major trouble.

"Can we go now?" Olympia asks, apparently unfazed at the reality of being expelled.

Miss Miriam looks down her nose at us. "Please do,"

she says, acid-tongued. "I cannot stand to look at either of you for one more minute."

Olympia flounces from the office. I follow.

We make it up to our room, whereupon Olympia collapses onto her bed and starts complaining.

"What an old witch!" she moans. "My poppa's going to be major pissed; he hates it when I get thrown out of school and he has to come get me and make nice and apologize for his naughty little girlikins. He made me swear I wouldn't get thrown out of this one. Shit!"

I can sympathize. Gino is not going to be exactly thrilled. But then he won't come to fetch me, he'll send someone— hopefully Marco.

Yes, the sad truth is that I still have a dumb girl crush on handsome Marco. It's pathetic, I know, only I can't help it.

"Well," Olympia says with a weary sigh. "I guess it'll be fathers' day tomorrow. What a trip!"

"My dad won't come," I say dourly. "He'll send someone."

"Why won't he come?" Olympia demands.

"'Cause he's a busy man," I explain.

"They're all busy."

"My old man's busier than most."

"Doing what?"

"Stuff," I answer vaguely. "Gino has a ton of interests. Hotels . . . companies . . . business things. You name it, he has a piece of it."

Olympia sits up. "Does he have a piece of Marabelle Blue?" she asks slyly.

I am completely startled. "How long have you known?" I ask, wide-eyed.

Olympia yawns and stretches as if it's no big deal. "A while," she murmurs. "I was waiting for *you* to tell me."

"Gino made me swear I wouldn't tell anyone," I mumble, slightly panicked. "He thinks if anyone finds out who I really am, they'll steer clear of me."

"As if," Olympia snorts. "I wish *my* father was a notorious gangster instead of a boring old billionaire."

"No you don't," I say firmly.

"Yes, I *do*," Olympia insists, wrinkling her nose. "And while we're on the subject . . . when do I get to meet the infamous Gino?" She pauses, gives me a secretive look, then lowers her voice. "I've read all about him. Tell me the truth—has he really arranged to have people killed?"

"That's so much crap," I snap. "Everything written about Gino is exaggerated."

"Okay," Olympia says, backing off because she can see I'm getting agitated.

And I am, because what do I know? Not much. I'm hardly naive when it comes to my father—I'm well aware he's not exactly citizen number one—but has he arranged to have people killed? No freaking way.

Olympia jumps off her bed and envelops me in a warm hug. I immediately feel comforted.

"I don't really care who your father is," she whispers in my ear. "You're my best friend, Lucky, and you always will be."

CHAPTER THIRTEEN

"Here comes trouble," Olympia exclaims as she almost falls leaning out of our window. "I think I spy your old man arriving."

"You do?" I gasp.

"Yes. And, hey, wait a minute—he's not so old, in fact he's hot!"

I feel a shiver of apprehension as I rush to join her at the window. Yes. It is Gino. Big surprise.

I can't make up my mind whether I am disappointed or elated.

Disappointed because I'd expected Marco. Elated because Daddy Dearest has actually made the trip. Which means he must care, a true shocker.

"Hmm . . ." says Olympia, leaving the window and running to admire herself in the mirror. "How do I look?"

"Who gives a crap how you look," I say brusquely. "Gino is actually here."

"That means I get to meet him," Olympia says, still primping.

"This isn't a social occasion," I point out. "We're about to get thrown out of school, remember?"

"In that case I should definitely look my best," Olympia giggles, thrusting out her boobs.

"Stop it!" I admonish.

"Spoilsport," Olympia retaliates.

A knock on our door and I am informed that I should go downstairs to the principal's office immediately.

No Marco to save me. Only Gino the Ram. Daddy Dearest. What'll he have to say?

Am I scared?

Not really. I am a Santangelo just like him. I am strong in my own way. I am powerful. I am woman!

Of course I crumble like a weakling when I come face to face with Gino. He is angry and handsome. Olympia is right—my father *is* hot with his thick black hair and intense dark eyes, impeccably dressed in an Italian hand-tailored suit and crisp white shirt.

Gino the Ram. Women lust after him. Women love him. I wish they wouldn't.

He gives me a look. *The* look that says—"So you screwed up again, huh? Can't you do anything right?"

"Hey . . . Daddy," I venture, playing little girl lost.

Maybe he'll call me princess and tell me all is forgiven.

"You packed?" he snarls, with about as much fatherly love as a snake.

"Yes, I'm packed," I say, throwing him a defiant glare. I haven't seen him in ages—don't I even get a hug?

No way. It's Gino the Ram. He's mad at me.

I can't even figure out why *he's* come to collect me. Surely he'd find it more convenient to send one of his lackeys? Marco, for instance.

Ah yes, Marco. I wouldn't mind seeing his face when Miss Miriam informs him I was caught naked in bed with a boy. Ha! Perhaps he'd finally see me as a real woman, experienced and very sexy.

No such luck—Gino is here and I have to deal with him.

"We should take off," Gino says to Miss Miriam.

I can tell by his tone of voice that he's way pissed off. Trouble lies ahead.

"Yes, perhaps you should," replies Miss Miriam, thin lips clamped tightly together.

"I appreciate your understanding," Gino says. "I'll be sendin' you that contribution for the school."

What contribution? Is he paying for her silence so she doesn't spill about his naughty little daughter? Me? Typical.

Ten minutes later we're sitting in a chauffeur-driven car on our way to the airport.

Gino is silent. So am I.

We board the plane in silence. Make the trip in silence. What was the point of him coming to get me if he has nothing to say?

The plane flies us to New York, not L.A. I am surprised. Why New York? L.A. is home.

I soon find out.

My father has an apartment in New York that I've never seen before. It's like something out of one of those men's magazines—all sleek and glam with an incredible sound system and mind-blowing views over Central Park. I guess I can get used to it.

I am thinking about how I'm going to enjoy New York, when Aunt Jen appears, all quivering lips and sympathetic hugs. "Hello, dear," she says, plump and motherly in a salmon-pink outfit with pearls galore. She smells of a musky scent, and has an expression on her face as if she's about to burst into tears. At least she's speaking to me, which is a relief.

"What are *you* doing here?" I ask.

"Gino requested that I come."

"He did?" I say, still trying to figure everything out.

"Indeed he did," she replies.

"Is Daddy still engaged?" I ask.

"Not anymore," Aunt Jen says crisply. "Miss Blue is history."

I digest this little piece of information. No more Marabelle Blue. Thank goodness. At least I don't have to deal with a movie-star psycho stepmom.

"Come, dear," Aunt Jen says. "Let us go in the bedroom and talk. There is nothing better than a thorough chat about things to clear the air."

I sigh. Do I really have to hash things out with Aunt Jen? How embarrassing.

"You do know that your father is *very* concerned about you," Aunt Jen says.

I glance over at Gino. He's at the bar, fixing himself what I presume is a strong drink. He still hasn't spoken to me.

I guess a conversation with Aunt Jen is inevitable. She's a sweet woman, but she's sure as hell not my mother.

Reluctantly I follow her, and we go into what I presume is Gino's bedroom. The room has my father's taste; it's all leather and dark wood—totally macho. Very suitable for Gino the Ram.

Aunt Jen perches herself daintily on the edge of the bed, whereupon she launches into an awkward speech about how girls have to save themselves for the boy they're eventually going to marry, and how above all else they must hang on to their self-respect and must never do anything untoward.

I get what she's after. She's desperate to find out—at Gino's request—exactly how far I have gone.

I give her what she needs to hear: "It was a one-time thing, Auntie Jen," I explain, all wide-eyed and innocent. "It's not as if we *did* anything. I'm still a good girl; the boy in my bed was a crazy lapse of judgment. I promise it'll never happen again."

Aunt Jen sighs with relief. She can now report back to Daddy Dearest that his precious little Italian princess is still a virgin.

After she imparts this piece of news to Gino, he summons me into the living room and begins to talk to me.

"Hey, kid," he says, "got somethin' planned for you."

"What?" I ask suspiciously.

"Somethin' you're gonna like," he replies, all cheerful and upbeat.

"Really?" I say, brightening up, because if he's happy I suppose I should be, too.

"Yeah, really."

"What?" I repeat, anxious to hear my fate.

Gino settles himself in an armchair, ready to tell me what I hope is going to be exciting news, although I have a lurking hunch it won't be.

"I'm sendin' you to a private boardin' school in Connecticut," he announces, like he's expecting me to jump up and down with joy.

My stomach takes a dive. So does my face.

"Now don't go givin' me one of your shitty looks," Gino grumbles, narrowing his eyes. "It's a great place. Oh yeah, an' it's closer to L.A., which means you get to fly home once a month, that's if ya feel like it. They got tennis, swimmin', an' ridin'—you like horses, doncha?"

"Horses!" I exclaim in horror. "I *hate* horses."

"C'*mon*, kiddo," Gino says, and I can hear it in his voice that he's getting fed up with the conversation. "Hate is kinda a strong way t'feel about horses—ya know, man's best friend an' all that crap."

"Dogs are man's best friend," I point out.

"No, money is man's best friend," Gino says, as usual determined to get the last word. "An' doncha forget it."

And there you have it. Not family. Not love. Money.
Gino the Ram. My father.

I hate him. He's brash, short, speaks poorly, and is coarse and full of his own importance.

I love him. He's handsome, macho, beautifully dressed, sexy—and when he's nice, he's very very nice.

Dinner is served. Now it's just me and Gino—Aunt Jen has conveniently vanished, her job well done.

I pick up an asparagus tip and lick the dripping butter with my tongue. "I was thinking . . ." I venture.

"Yeah?" says Gino, one eye firmly fixed on a ball game playing on TV.

"Umm . . . well . . . I mean . . . in a couple of months I'm going to be sixteen," I say. "So why do I have to go back to school at all?"

"Huh?"

I haven't quite got his full attention, but almost.

"Here's the thing," I continue quickly. "You know that I hate school, and school obviously hates me. And it's not as if I ever learn anything, so basically it's a total waste of time. *And* a waste of your money," I add, thinking this might encourage him to back off the private school idea. Hey—I've been thrown out of one, isn't that enough?

Gino gives me a long steady look.

Yippee! I finally have his full attention.

"No school, huh?" he growls. "An' what exactly would you be plannin' t'do all day?"

Wow! Is he actually taking me seriously? I can't believe it.

"I was thinking I could follow you around, learn everything about the family business," I say eagerly. "You do so many things, and maybe you can teach me."

"Teach you, huh?"

"Yes," I say, my words tumbling over each other as I struggle to impress him. "I pick things up real quick. I can be your right hand. I can learn all about Vegas and the hotel business."

"Jesus Christ!" Gino suddenly explodes. "What are you—delusional?"

"No, just smart, like you," I mutter stubbornly.

"Forget about it, kid. You're a girl. Education's what you need. You're gonna finish school, go to college, meet a nice guy, get married, an' have a bunch of kids. Sounds like a plan t'me."

"Sounds lousy to me," I respond, holding back angry tears. "When you talk like that it sounds as if you've got one foot in the last century."

"Y'know something, you have yourself a real smart mouth, Lucky," Gino says, his black eyes growing even darker with anger.

Wow! His words are mirroring Marco's. Just because I have something to say for myself, does that mean that I have a smart mouth? What utter crap.

"Take a long look at me, kiddo," Gino continues. "I never had no fancy private education. I was out bustin' my ass to make a buck long before I was your age."

Yes, Daddy, I know. You've told me countless times.

"You—kiddo—are gettin' everythin' I never had. So whyn't you shut the fuck up, an' remember how fortunate you are."

Thanks, Daddy. What a lovely fatherly speech.

"So here's the deal," Gino mutters. "You'll do as I say, an' one of these days you're gonna kiss my ass an' thank me. Got it?"

CHAPTER FOURTEEN

"New girl . . . new girl . . . new girl." Everywhere I go I hear the whispers. Yes, I *am* indeed the new girl—however, I do not fit the image of the other girls. Most of them are uptight white girls with hair neatly tied back, no makeup, and pristine uniforms. I stand out with my wild black curls, deep olive skin, and touches of mascara and lip gloss. I have also adapted the school uniform to suit me. I have shortened the skirt, unbuttoned the blouse, and abandoned the tie. A far better look.

Within days I am summoned to the principal's office, another tight-ass with major attitude.

Here we go again, I think.

Thanks, Gino, for sending me somewhere I hate.

"We have an extremely strict dress code here," the principal, a woman with a vast expanse of forehead and large horse teeth, informs me. "And we certainly do *not* allow our girls to wear makeup."

"Lip gloss isn't makeup," I object. "That's stupid."

And for those few words I get detention, which is not all bad because detention takes place in an outer building, and directly outside the building I observe a young Mexican gardener doing his thing. Well, he's not exactly doing his thing—that sounds rude—he's actually sweeping up leaves and looking quite pissed off about it.

Once I've written *Lip gloss is makeup* five hundred times, I make my way outside to maybe get acquainted with the gardener. I soon discover that his name is Lopez, that he works for his father, and he is twenty. He's also major cute, with flashing eyes almost as dark as mine, extremely long eyelashes, and a dangerous scar running down his left cheek.

I ask him how he got the scar. He tells me he was in a gang until his father whisked him out of the Bronx to the greenery and calmness of Connecticut.

I am impressed, and slightly excited. We arrange to meet later, and he fills me in on the safest window to escape from.

I like Lopez. He's my kind of guy.

Am I boy crazy?

A bit.

Why not? It's all part of growing up.

Lopez and I enjoy three nights of unbridled lust ("almost" still in play) until Miranda, a sour-faced girl with a righteous attitude who bunks in my dorm room, gives us up.

Lopez is fired.

I get detention.

Here we go again.

I realize the time has come to make a daring escape.

Later that night I think things through. Where is Olympia? What is she up to?

Once again she will be my salvation. I know it.

~ ~ ~

I think I have inherited my dad's street smarts along with his looks. I do look just like him, only I'm taller. I enjoy being tall and lean, and it's fortunate for me that I can pass for at least eighteen or nineteen, 'cause this makes my flight to freedom so much easier.

Olympia comes through as usual. I track her down via phone to Paris, where she is holed up in her father's Avenue Foch apartment, taking a Russian language course, which she informs me she hates. Thrilled to hear from me, she arranges to get me a plane ticket to France, then she has a male friend phone the school pretending to be Gino, saying there is a family emergency and that I have to leave immediately.

Quite frankly I don't think anyone is at all sorry to see me go, especially Miranda, who gives me a triumphant snarl of a smile and a fake "Have fun at your next school. We'll all *really* miss you here."

A typical mean girl. I wish her nothing but the worst.

The plane ride to France is uneventful. Olympia is at the airport in Paris to meet me. We hug and kiss and giggle at the insanity of it all. Then we walk outside, and to my surprise Olympia jumps behind the wheel of a cool white Mercedes convertible.

"Wow!" I exclaim, throwing my suitcase in the back.

"'Wow' is right," Olympia says, grinning broadly. "Not bad, huh?"

"Who does this car belong to?"

"Dear old Mom," Olympia says. "She never drives it—besides, she's never here—so I have taken possession. Right now we're off on a magical mystery tour, so I suggest you hold on to your knickers!"

"Where are we going?" I ask, drinking in the heady taste of freedom.

"South of France," Olympia says, as if it's the most normal place to run off to. "I got it all figured out. One of my aunts has a villa above Cannes. She *never* goes there, so it'll be all shuttered up. The good news is that I know how to get in, 'cause I used to spend the summers there with my nanny when my dear old parents didn't have time for me, which was mostly every summer."

"How will you explain this to your family?"

"You think they care? No way. It's just me and a housekeeper in the Paris apartment. I told her I had to go see my mom, and since the old crow doesn't speak English, she couldn't care less. Which means we are free—on our own—and ready to have an incredible adventure. Right?"

I couldn't agree more. The two of us against the world. I like it!

Olympia is the perfect friend, she always comes through when I need her. What more can one ask of a friendship?

Naturally she drives like a maniac.

"You're a crazy driver," I gulp, hanging on. "I didn't know you even had a driver's license."

"Don't," Olympia replies matter-of-factly. "Let's hope we're not stopped." She swerves to avoid an old man crossing the street. He shakes his fist at her. She turns on the radio, blasts it loud, and gives him the finger.

I cling to the side of my seat. This is insane, but I'm loving it!

"How far's the South of France?" I ask, attempting to remain cool.

"Not far," Olympia replies. "Shouldn't take us more than a day or two."

A day or two! I am speechless. Yet I am also excited. So what if she drives like a crazy person? This is our adventure, and I am totally into it.

Eight hours later I am not so sure. We're in a convertible and the sun is relentlessly beating down on us as we drive across France. I am thirsty and sweaty and starving hungry.

"Don't you think we should stop somewhere?" I suggest.

Olympia shrugs and points out that we don't have a lot of cash between us.

"What about your credit card?" I say.

"Hmm . . ." Olympia replies. "I guess we can use it."

"Why not?"

"Don't want to leave a trail of where we are."

"It'll be fine," I say, desperate for a break.

"You're right," Olympia agrees. "Nobody's going to be checking on us."

Ten minutes later we pull into a dusty Novotel and book a room. I fall onto the bed and into a deep sleep, too tired to even think about eating.

When I finally awake it is dark out and there's no Olympia in sight.

Where is she? I think, exasperated. *Foraging for food, I hope.* My stomach is groaning with hunger.

I make it out to the motel swimming pool, a depressing oasis surrounded by concrete, a couple of sad palm trees, and one solitary light.

Olympia is in the pool making out with a boy I've never seen before. She is topless.

Hey—I'm also into boys, but not random pickups at some anonymous motel.

"What's up?" I say, trying not to sound like the uptight friend.

"What isn't?" Olympia giggles. "Meet Pierre—he doesn't speak English, so we're communicating via the language of love."

French Pierre surfaces with a stupid leer on his face.

Oh crap! Olympia is way out of control.

CHAPTER FIFTEEN

What have I gotten myself into? The next morning Olympia is nowhere in sight and her bed hasn't been slept in. I take a shower under a rusty faucet, dress quickly, and head downstairs. A couple of French families are sitting out by the pool complete with ratty little kids running riot around the edge. Food and drink is available from a vending machine. I get a bag of chips and an Orangina. Then I go check on Olympia's Mercedes, which is exactly where she left it. Doesn't take much street smarts to realize she must've spent the night with French boy.

When they finally appear around noon, I see that French boy is hardly a boy. He looks to be about thirty-something with a scraggly ginger beard and scrawny arms. Whatever happened to hot?

"Sorry," Olympia giggles, obviously not sorry at all. "We kinda slept in, if you know what I mean."

French Pierre squeezes her arm and plants a wet kiss on her cheek.

I get the feeling that maybe Olympia has stopped practicing "almost," and is possibly going all the way. This is not good news, for I have no intention of going all the way with anyone, and if Olympia's doing it, will she expect me to follow?

"Shouldn't we get going?" I say, giving Olympia a meaningful look.

"What's your hurry?" she responds, clinging to Pierre as if he's some kind of sex god.

"I thought we could get there by tonight," I argue. "Isn't that what we planned?"

"Yes," Olympia answers vaguely. "But that was before I met Pierre."

Oh crap. Olympia's in love again. She goes through crushes like Kleenex.

I am stuck for words. I am in Olympia's car on my way to Olympia's aunt's house. I have no money and no power. I am not only stuck for words, I am well and truly stuck.

I vow that I will never allow myself to be caught in this position again. Olympia is calling all the shots, and I am tagging along like a stupid little puppy dog.

What to do?

Nothing. There is nothing I *can* do.

I am pissed. I feel a dark rage boiling up inside me. I

think I have Gino's temper. I have seen him explode and it's not a pretty sight.

On the other hand, staying calm will probably get me further. Fighting with Olympia is a bad option. Like I said—she has the power.

So I swallow my frustration and play along. Which means watching Olympia and French Pierre making out on a sunbed, until one of the rugrat kids running around the pool trips over Pierre's feet, which are limply hanging off the end of the sunbed.

Pierre leaps up, roars with fury, and begins screaming at the kid in French.

The kid, no more than five or six, freezes, allowing Pierre to grab him by the scruff of his neck and begin shaking him.

The kid starts crying, and since it looks as if no one's going to do anything, I launch into action. I am on my feet Santangelo-style.

"Leave the boy alone!" I yell at Pierre. "Can't you see it was an accident?"

Pierre is not listening. He seems to be taking some kind of sadistic pleasure in shaking the little boy as hard as he can. I am stunned.

Without thinking it through, I run at Pierre and grab his long stringy hair until he is forced to let go of the boy. However, Pierre is not finished—as the kid runs off, he turns on me and slaps me hard across the face, shouting some kind of insult.

"For God's sake!" Olympia shouts, finally jumping up. "Stop it!"

Pierre ignores her and goes to hit me again, at which point I grab his wrist, twist it, and issue a sharp kick to his saggy balls.

He lets out a yelp of pain and turns to Olympia for comfort.

She gives him a scornful look, tosses back her long blonde hair, and says a very succinct "S'long, asshole."

Ten minutes later we are in the car and on our merry way.

~ ~ ~

Now here we are, back on the road. Olympia can't wait to reveal all the gruesome details of her one-nighter with French Pierre. I'm not sure I want to hear.

To change the subject I fan myself with a magazine and say, "It's so hot! I bet we both stink. Two stinky little virgins."

"Hmm . . ." Olympia says, blonde hair flying in the breeze. "You might want to correct that statement."

"Huh?"

"I was going to tell you when we got to the house. Y'know, like sitting around the pool sipping white wine. But yeah, last night I did the deed for the second time."

"The second time," I say, quite startled. "Who was the first?"

"Oh, some commie French bastard," Olympia says vaguely. "He kept on lecturing me that my father should be shot, and that I didn't know anything."

"Sounds like a real charmer."

"Yeah, right. Like a fool I smuggled him into the Paris apartment one night, and he refused to settle for 'almost.' So I did the deed. Silly me. I hated every vile minute of it."

"You did?" I ask, wondering why she did it again if she hated it so much.

Olympia glances over at me and wrinkles her nose. "It was horrible!" she exclaims. "Stick to 'almost,' it's much more enjoyable."

I decide now is not the time to question her more. Better she should concentrate on her driving—which is still appalling.

I sit back and begin thinking about Gino's words to me. "You're gonna finish school, go to college, get married, have kids, an' settle down."

No, Daddy Dearest, I am certainly not. I want a life, a career. I want to be powerful and respected. I want to build hotels like you. I want in on the family business. I might be a girl, but I can do anything a boy can do. You'll see. You'll get it.

As these thoughts are drifting through my head, Olympia announces that we are practically there.

We turn off the freeway onto a narrow road hewn out

of rock. We are parallel with the blue Mediterranean and sandy beaches. It all looks blissful.

"This is gonna be so fab," Olympia says with a happy sigh. "Prepare yourself for a crapload of good times!"

Oh yes, I am totally prepared.

CHAPTER SIXTEEN

Set high in the hills above Cannes, Olympia's aunt's villa is closed to all intruders. This does not deter Olympia, who jumps from the car and forces the huge wrought-iron gates open so that she can drive the Mercedes up to the house. I am excited—this is indeed an adventure.

The villa itself is painted pink with closed wooden shutters on all the windows, and incredible gardens filled with bougainvillea, mimosa, and jasmine. The smell of the flowers is overwhelming.

"How're we getting in?" I ask tentatively.

"No prob," Olympia says, once again leaping out of the car. "There's a broken catch on an upstairs window; all I gotta do is climb a tree and we're in!"

Olympia is nothing if not resourceful; she's also the queen of "no prob." I watch as she shimmies up a tall peach tree, springs the shutter, opens the window, and climbs in. A few minutes later she opens up the front door from the inside and ushers me in. "Welcome to Casa Good Times," she says, grinning broadly. "We are the new tenants!"

My sense of what an adventure this is revs into overdrive. I am actually in the South of France—a school runaway, and nobody knows where I am! I feel totally free.

Take that, Gino. Girls can do anything.

The villa is an amazing place with many rooms filled with furniture covered in dustsheets and more than a few cobwebs here and there. Out back is a leaf-strewn swimming pool surrounded by several lounge chairs with plastic covers.

"My aunt only uses this place a couple of weeks a year," Olympia reveals, starting to pull off some of the dustsheets. "The work force moves in a couple of weeks before she does. Do you realize we could probably stay here for months before anyone finds us? Nobody would ever dream of looking for us here."

Hmm . . . I hadn't actually imagined being on the missing list for months. Gino will have a shit-fit if he can't find me—that's if he ever discovers I'm missing.

Or maybe not. Does he even care? Who knows? I certainly don't.

While I mull this over, Olympia checks out the kitchen and discovers that the refrigerator is stocked with wine, beer, and 7-Up. A walk-in cupboard offers caterers' boxes of potato chips, cans of tuna fish, and multiple packets of nuts. No other food in sight.

"Okay," Olympia decides. "Tonight we head into town and get ourselves a decent meal. I don't know about you, but I fancy a great big bowl of bouillabaisse and some fresh lobster smothered in mayonnaise. Sounds yummy."

"Can we afford it?" I ask, thinking of our somewhat meager funds.

Olympia throws me one of her looks. "Who needs money when we've got our fine young bodies?" she says with her usual giggle. "Guys will be *gagging* to buy us dinner."

~ ~ ~

It occurs to me that Olympia is always right. She sure knows her stuff, because the moment we hit the main drag in Cannes, guys are all over us! Well, I guess I should say guys are all over Olympia. It's the big boobs and the blonde hair, not to mention the short shorts she has squeezed herself into, so short that they barely cover her ass.

I suppose we make an odd couple—me in my tight jeans and T-shirt, Olympia dressed to kill. I could show off my bod if I wanted to, the thing is—I don't want to.

Olympia boldly checks out the prospects, finally settling on a slim blondish man who is sitting by himself on the Blue Bar terrace. He gets up when she passes for the second time, mumbles something about haven't they met before, then when she says no way—he invites us both for a drink.

I am inclined to say no. However, Olympia is already sitting down at his table, and he is ordering Pernod all around.

Reluctantly I join her, even though I'm not sure I like the look of him. He strikes me as a bit shifty with his long corn-colored hair and pale eyelashes.

It turns out he's an American film producer by the name of Warris Charters, and he's in town for the Cannes Film Festival.

"What films have you produced?" I ask, wondering if food is on the agenda.

His eyes switch from Olympia's boobs to me.

"*Kiss and Kill*," he says brusquely. "Big hit."

"Never heard of it," I want to say, only I don't. Seems he's the one about to buy us dinner so I'd better stay cool.

"I wouldn't mind being an actress," Olympia says, flashing him a winning smile. "Maybe you'll put me in one of your movies."

"Acting's not all glitz and glamour," Warris remarks, scratching his chin. "I was a child star until I hit puberty. At thirteen it was all over—so eventually I turned producer. Control and cash, that's where it's all at."

Olympia's face lights up. She is already into him, I can tell.

"Where are you girls from?" Warris asks.

"We're international," Olympia replies, sipping her champagne.

I can see Warris thinking. He knows we're young, and he must be wondering how come we're on the loose in Cannes. He has to be at least thirty—old, like Marco. Only Marco is deliciously dark and sexy and Warris is so not. I wish I was with Marco now.

"I'm starving," Olympia announces. "Can we order food?"

"Great idea," I say, happily joining in.

Warris leans closer to Olympia and whispers something in her ear. I strain to hear. He's tempting her with grass instead of food. Bummer! I've tried pot a couple of times, and I'm not sure I enjoy feeling out of control.

"Where can we go?" Olympia asks, and I know she's hoping that Warris has his own yacht or something along those lines. Olympia is all for luxury unlimited.

Warris shrugs and says, "Where are *you* staying? My hotel doesn't encourage visitors."

Huh?

Much to my annoyance, Olympia buys his bullshit. "We have a villa in the hills," she says, like we haven't vowed to keep our whereabouts a deep dark secret. "We can go there."

Bad move. We don't know anything about this lechy-looking guy, and now we're taking him home with us. Not the coolest move in the world.

"Let's go," Warris says. "I'll grab us a cab."

"No need," Olympia boasts. "I have a car."

"Yeah?" Warris says, duly impressed. Even more so when he gets sight of the white Mercedes parked on the street.

Olympia flicks him the keys. "You drive," she says, as if they're an old married couple.

And off we go.

CHAPTER SEVENTEEN

So here we are at the villa with Olympia's soon-to-be new best friend, Warris Charters, a man I don't trust at all—he of the shifty pale blue eyes and shallow expression. Warris is in possession of primo grass. Olympia is thrilled, especially when he starts paying her a ton of attention, which is exactly what she craves. Once again I am more or less ignored, because when it comes to me or a potential conquest, Olympia is all about the latest male presence. I'm beginning to realize loyalty is not her strong suit.

Warris is wandering from room to room, taking it all in. "Is this place yours?" he asks Olympia.

I can see dollar signs flicking in his beady eyes.

"It belongs to my family," she replies airily, before leading him out to the pool.

I trail behind them, determined not to be left out. Why, I don't know—it's not as if I'm even remotely interested in this Warris Charters person. Maybe it's 'cause I don't trust him, therefore I don't think I should leave Olympia alone with him. When it comes to men it's obvious that Olympia is totally gullible.

The outside pool lights don't work, so Olympia runs back inside and returns with candles and a bottle of wine.

Warris fires up a joint, and after taking a long drag hands it on to Olympia, who then passes it to me.

Like I said, I've tried pot twice before, both times with Olympia. Now, what the hell—here I go again . . .

After what seems like hours or possibly only a few minutes, Olympia jumps up from her lounge chair, strips off all her clothes, flashes her boobs at Warris, and leaps into the pool stark naked. Talk about not waiting around for the getting-to-know-you period!

A delighted Warris is not slow to follow. Off come his pants and shirt and he immediately dives in after her.

By this time I am totally stoned, which is why I feel relaxed enough to whip off my jeans and top. Then I realize there is no point, because Olympia and Warris are already at it in the pool, and not wishing to be a third wheel I wander back into the house and begin searching for something to eat.

Tuna, anyone?

I devour an entire can of the oily fish, then stagger off to bed. Apparently nobody is about to miss me.

Maybe life on the run is not all it's cracked up to be.

~ ~ ~

In the morning Olympia is once again on the missing list. She is not in the bedroom we decided to share. I suspect she is somewhere with Warris.

My stomach drops. Is this to be a repeat of our motel stop? Is Warris next in line after French Pierre?

I am verging on furious, because this is supposed to be me and her against the world, and I have a sinking feeling that Warris is a relentless hanger-on. He will not be as easy to get rid of as French Pierre.

I set off to find them, and there they are in the master bedroom sprawled nude and fast asleep on the big bed.

So much for fun times in the sun, just me and Olympia, two best friends enjoying a big adventure. I don't think so. I have a nasty hunch that Warris is here to stay.

I make it to the kitchen, where I locate coffee and a percolator. No food. Gotta hit a market today before I starve to death.

The two of them do not emerge until noon. Is this a pattern? Olympia, bleary-eyed with a stupid smile on her face. Warris, looking mighty pleased with himself, his yellow hair flopping on his forehead, baggy shorts covering something large that I do not wish to see. Ugh! Gross! He has skinny white legs with flabby calf muscles. Double gross!

At least the boys I've chosen to have fun with have been major hot.

For a moment I reflect on my conquests. Not a bad list. First the boys we liaised with on our nighttime sojourns from L'Evier—especially Ursi, whom I guess I should call my first real adventure. Then Brad—not my favorite memory. And of course Brandon, followed closely by Jack—the Kissing King—then English Chad, the reason I got kicked out of school. And finally Lopez, the gardener's son, quite the stud. Not a bad list.

Once again I consider the fact that I am a woman of experience, even though I have not gone all the way with any of them. I am truly beginning to understand men. Keep 'em wanting more, that's the secret.

"Hey," Olympia says with a vague note of surprise. "You're up."

Where the hell does she expect me to be? Still sleeping in my lonely bed?

This is such crap. I throw her one of my willful glares. She ignores it and clings to Warris.

There are times I feel like I'm in the wrong place at the wrong time. There are moments I cannot stand Olympia and the way she flirts, sticks out her boobs, and expects every man to fall at her feet.

I hate being a year younger than her—I cannot wait to be sixteen, because sixteen is a magical age. You're no longer a kid, and therefore cannot be treated like one.

I have plans, big plans. I refuse to live my life through boys as Olympia does. Oh yes, they can be fun and challenging—but as a full-time occupation, I think not. I want so much more. I want to build hotels like Gino, run big businesses, I want to be a force of nature, a leader, a woman who counts in this world. My name is Lucky Santangelo, not Lucky Saint. *I want to be heard!* And you can bet on it—I will be.

"Wassup?" Olympia says, yawning. "You look pissed."

I shake my head. Never give anyone the satisfaction of knowing how you truly feel—I heard Gino say that once and I reckon he's right.

"We should stock up on food," I say, keeping it in neutral.

"Great plan," Warris says. "Let's go get supplies, then maybe I'll ask some of my friends over."

Olympia nods. I can see she's still half stoned. She looks like crap, with mussed-up hair and yesterday's makeup caked on her face.

"Is there a market near here?" I ask.

"We'll find one," Warris says. "D'you drive?"

"Yes," I boldly reply.

Olympia shoots me a look as if to say "Really?"

Last night she told Warris that she's nineteen and I'm eighteen. I don't think he'd be psyched to find out that he's moved in on two underage girls—runaways at that. I can just imagine how Gino would deal with him. He'd cut off his balls and put 'em in a blender.

I stifle a giggle and wonder what Dimitri, Olympia's dad, would do. Probably ban him from whichever country he felt like banning him from. Dimitiri Stanislopoulos exudes power—a different kind of power than Gino, but power all the same.

Warris wanders off to take a shower and for a moment I have Olympia to myself.

"Tell me the deal," I demand. "Is he staying with us or what?"

A beatific smile crosses Olympia's face. "For as long as I want," she says, twirling a strand of blonde hair.

And apparently she wants.

CHAPTER EIGHTEEN

There is no market in the vicinity—only a twisting narrow street full of small neighborhood shops specializing in various cheeses, crusty loaves of bread, pâté, ham, and nothing much else. Warris of course finds a wine store and proceeds to stock up. When it comes time to pay he feigns dismay at not having his credit card with him. What an a-hole. Surely Olympia will catch on?

She doesn't. She pays up with a stupid smile still plastered all over her face. Then she manages to whisper to me in a reverent tone, "Oh my God! He's such a stud in bed!" Which makes me want to barf.

I realize that I am trapped with the two of them. The American hustler (oh yes, I've got his number) and the Greek heiress, for Olympia has informed me on numerous occasions that one day she will inherit the Stanislopoulos fortune—or at least her share. If only Warris knew, he would probably propose on the spot.

I wonder how I can escape from the two of them, at least get to spend the day by myself. I do not fancy watching them make out by the pool again—it's not what I ran away to do.

After we get back to the villa and stuff our faces, I casually suggest that I take the Mercedes out for a drive.

Olympia, who has taken to walking around topless— her huge boobs in everyone's faces—seems to think it's a great idea.

Sure she does. *Let's get rid of the annoying friend who's getting in my way.*

Knowing Olympia, I get that's what she's thinking.

Warris, however, does not condone me taking the car unless I can have it back within a couple of hours. "I might have to go into town for an important movie meeting," he explains to Olympia, all puffed up with his own importance.

I hate his smug face with its pale eyelashes and worm-like lips. But I, too, know how to play the game. "Sure," I say with an agreeable nod. "I'll be back soon."

And so I make my escape. Phew! A shaky mistake 'cause I've never driven a Mercedes before—just one of the family cars, and that was only a few times.

I feel powerful and slightly terrified at the same time.

I proceed slowly, like a snail, with no idea where I'm headed.

Another adventure. All mine.

Eventually I make it down to the coastal road, cleverly

missing a Renault and a Citroën. Both drivers scream ob-
scenities at me. I ignore them and make a sharp left, then
I keep going until I reach a resort town with the sign
Juan-les-Pins.

Seems like a good place to stop, so I find a parking
place and gingerly wedge the Mercedes between two cars.
It's snug, but at least I haven't hit anything.

I am triumphant. Marco should only see me now, driving around the South of France by myself.

Actually, I wish I wasn't by myself. Aren't adventures
supposed to be shared? Wasn't that the plan? Me and
Olympia out on our own discovering life.

Too bad Olympia's a raving nympho.

Juan-les-Pins is a small, active beach community—lots
of little shops and plenty of young people milling around.
I stop at an open-air café located across from a book and
magazine stand, and bag a table. A hot young waiter asks
me in French what I want. I order a croissant and coffee.
He winks and compliments my T-shirt, which happens to
feature my favorite Rolling Stones.

I am so glad that Miss Bossy insisted I take language
courses; it certainly helps to speak the lingo.

I sit there for a while, allowing my mind to wander.

What's going to happen next? If Warris is about to become a permanent fixture, I want out. But how does that
come about? Nobody knows where I am. I have hardly any
money—certainly not enough for a ticket home. Not to
mention the fact that Gino will be double pissed when he

CONFESSIONS OF A WILD CHILD | 107

discovers I dumped school and took off. Seems as if I'm trapped.

Young hot waiter keeps on refilling my coffee cup. He's definitely a babe, with dirty blond sticking-up hair and a cheeky grin. He's also my height, which is not exactly my type, but right now I'll settle for a friendly face.

"Are you English?" he asks after a while.

"American," I reply, surprised that he has no accent. "And you?"

"Half French, half Scottish, and I'm off in an hour, so maybe I can show you around."

Oh yeah, you can certainly show me around. Sounds like a fine plan. Besides, I've got nothing else to do.

"I'm Jon," he offers.

"I'm Lucky," I say.

Jon winks at me. "No, *I'm* the lucky one," he says with a crooked grin.

We'll see . . .

~ ~ ~

We stroll all around Juan-les-Pins. Jon is funny and inter-esting and about as unlike slimy Warris as anyone could be. He tells me that he's studying economics in Paris, and spending his summer making money to support himself.

"The tourists tip well," he explains. "Especially when I turn on the charm."

"Is that what you did with me?" I ask jokingly.

"A little bit," he says with a sly grin. "Only *you* didn't tip me."

"That's 'cause you refused to give me a check," I counter. "How could I?"

"You're too beautiful for me to charge you."

Beautiful! Nobody has ever called me that before. For once I am speechless and kind of caught off guard. Jon has way too much charm and I'm eating it up.

We end up on the beach making out. Why not?

I like the way he kisses—every boy seems to have a different technique, and Jon's is pretty good.

Am I becoming an expert at kissing? I haven't had any complaints.

Ah, Marco, by the time we get together I will be an experienced woman of the world. How does that grab you?

After a while I decide that if Olympia can have slimy Warris at the villa, then I can certainly invite Jon over. So I do.

"I'm working tonight," he says with a rueful shrug. "How about tomorrow? I'm off all day."

"Yes," I say, as he walks me to my car. "This doesn't belong to me," I add quickly as I note his reaction to the Mercedes. "It belongs to my friend's dad."

"And he lets you drive it?" Jon asks, sounding surprised.

"Why wouldn't he?" I respond, feeling a bit defensive.

"It's an expensive car," Jon remarks, circling it.

"That it is," I agree.

He leans me against the side of the car and kisses me hard. "Tomorrow, beautiful. What time?"

I catch my breath. "Anytime," I say vaguely. "We can swim, there's a pool."

Jon nods. *"Bonne nuit,* Lucky," he says, and before I know it I am driving confidently back to the villa.

CHAPTER NINETEEN

"Where the *fuck* have you been?" Warris explodes, red in the face. I take a quick peek at my watch and realize that it's almost seven P.M. *Too bad, Warris, I was out having fun.*

"Ran into some friends," I say casually.

"You fuckin' *what*?" Warris screams, his face getting redder by the minute. I glance around to see what Olympia is up to and if she's going to allow her newfound boyfriend to speak to me like this.

Olympia is draped on a couch smoking yet another joint. Olympia never does anything by halves. She is oblivious to what is going on.

"I missed an important meeting because of you," Warris steams. "I told you I needed the fucking car."

"Does your mom get to kiss you on that dirty mouth?" I say sharply.

"What did you say, bitch?" Warris demands.

I lose it. Nobody calls me a bitch and gets away with it. "You're an asshole," I snap. "And I'd sooner be a bitch than an asshole."

"I knew you were trouble," Warris yells. "It's written all over your wop face."

"Better to be trouble than an asshole," I taunt.

"Jesus Christ!" he says, steps close to me, and raises his arm as if to strike me.

I move quickly, faster than him. Uncle Costa taught me a few key moves when I was a kid, and I've never forgotten them. I grab Warris's arm, twist it back, and give him a swift kick in the balls.

He yells like a stuck pig and crumples to the ground. Talk about a wimp!

"Sorry," I say innocently. "Did I hurt you?"

Oh wow, I'm getting good at this—I recall Pierre and *his* demise. Maybe I should run a self-defense class. Go for the balls, it works every time!

Warris staggers to his feet and glares at me. "Your little friend is a raging psycho," he informs Olympia, who doesn't stir. She is in a world of her own—stoned and happy. "Fuckin' bitch!" Warris mutters, and I'm not sure if he's referring to me or Olympia. I guess he means me, 'cause he wouldn't risk alienating Olympia.

I make it to what I now consider my room, since Olympia has taken up residence with Warris in the main bedroom.

I lie down on the bed and stare at the old-fashioned ceiling fan. I think about Jon, he is kind of cute. I think about Marco and wonder what he's up to back in L.A. Does he ever think about me? Does my image even cross his mind?

I wish I was older. If I was older I could make money and start doing what *I* want to do. I wouldn't be trapped with Olympia in a house in the South of France with no clue about what happens next. Eventually Gino will get word that I'm on the run. He will not be pleased. One way or the other he will hunt me down.

I must've fallen asleep, 'cause it's dark when Olympia awakens me by shaking my shoulder.

"Wassup?" I mumble, rubbing my eyes.

"Get up and get dressed," Olympia insists. "Warris is taking us for a night on the town."

"You're kidding, right?" I say, still not thinking straight.

"Not kidding," Olympia assures me. "He's taking us to the casino."

I digest this news. Aren't we too young to gain entry to a casino?

I don't voice my opinion, because I'm quite into the idea of getting out of the house, even if it is with Warris.

~ ~ ~

An hour later we're sitting on the terrace of the Blue Bar, sipping Campari while all dressed up in Olympia's aunt's clothes. I have chosen a black sequinned tank top and palazzo pants. Olympia is wearing something extremely low cut—of course. She's never happy unless her boobs are on display.

Warris has decided to deposit us there while he runs over to his hotel and changes clothes. Olympia suggests we go with him, but he demurs.

"Well," she threatens, sticking out her boobs, "if I see a better-looking dude, do not expect me to be here when you get back."

Warris shoots her a confident smirk. He knows she likes him.

"Watch her," he says briskly. "I'll be no more than ten minutes."

It's obvious that he has decided I'm more use to him as a friend than as an enemy. Smarter than I thought.

It's kind of interesting sitting at a table observing a ton of old men with way younger girlfriends passing by. According to Warris, this is the height of the Cannes Film Festival, so there are lots of important movie people in town.

Who cares? I certainly don't.

After a good half hour Warris returns all dressed up in a white dinner jacket. He kisses Olympia on the mouth, and announces that he's checked out of his hotel and stashed his suitcase in the back of the Mercedes.

Olympia is unfazed.

I am pissed. The asshole is taking up permanent residence. No slouch when it comes to nailing the deal.

We finish our drinks and set off for the casino, whereupon we get stopped at the entrance by two burly French dudes in suits.

"Excuse me, monsieur," burly French dude one says to Warris, "I shall be needing identification for the two young ladies."

Warris bristles. "They're both over twenty-one," he says sharply.

"I am sure they are," the French dude replies with an implacable expression. "However, there are rules, and unless the young ladies can provide their passports I cannot allow them into the casino."

"Do you know who I am?" Warris snarls, his face reddening.

"I am sorry, monsieur, these are the rules we must follow. There are no exceptions."

Warris suddenly loses it. "Fucking frogs!" he screams. "What the fuck do you know about *anything*?"

"Oh God!" Olympia sighs. "It's not important. Let's go."

Warris is on a roll, screaming insults as two security guards materialize and, arms under his elbows, escort him off the premises.

"Wonderful!" I mutter as we reach the sidewalk, and as we do, a white Rolls-Royce pulls up, and out steps a fiery dark-haired Latina in an even tighter and more revealing dress than Olympia's. She is older, but quite a beauty.

"Warris!" the woman says accusingly, jabbing him with

her be-ringed finger. "Where the hell have you been? I've been searching for you everywhere."

Warris stops shouting, shakes off the two security guards, adjusts his jacket, and gives the woman a sheepish look. "Pippa," he mumbles. "I was going to call you."

"Sure," she replies sarcastically. "And the president took a shit in Washington Square."

Ha! I like this woman's style—she has a mouth on her. And I so enjoy seeing Warris crumble.

Olympia doesn't. She clings to Warris's arm in a proprietary fashion and demands to know who the dark-haired woman is.

"Pippa Sanchez," the woman says, looking Olympia up and down before turning back to Warris and drawling—"I didn't know juvenile pussy was your style. I guess all the *big* girls must've found out what a crap artist you are."

I am loving this. Totally loving it!

"Pippa," Warris says stiffly, "I'd like you to meet Olympia Stanislopoulos of *the* Stanislopoulos family."

"Oh!" Pippa says. I realize she gets it. Like Warris, she is no slouch.

"And Olympia," Warris continues, "I'd like *you* to meet Pippa Sanchez, a business associate of mine."

Business associate my left foot, I think, stifling a giggle.

Naturally Olympia falls for it, just as Pippa's escort steps forward. He is the driver of the Rolls, a gray-haired older man.

"Ah," the man says. "If these people are your friends, Pippa, we should all go have a drink together."

Pippa nods, flashes Warris a scathing look, and once again we are off.

CHAPTER TWENTY

The gray-haired man, whose name I soon discover is March Holtz, insists that we all pile into his Rolls, and since Warris obviously thinks the man might be someone important, he doesn't hesitate before hustling me and Olympia into the car. Warris crams in the back between me and Olympia. Pippa sits in the front passenger seat next to March. We leave the Mercedes parked in Cannes while March roars off down the narrow coastal road, announcing we are meeting up with more people at a club in Juan-les-Pins.

Juan-les-Pins again? Really? I wonder if I'll bump into Jon.

"I've been to Juan-les-Pins," I remark.

"When?" Olympia demands, bountiful boobs almost popping out of her aunt's low-cut purple dress.

"This afternoon," I say casually, and I want to add, *While you were lying around stoned with your new boyfriend when you should've been with me, having fun and enjoying our newfound freedom.* But I don't, 'cause there's no endgame to getting in a fight with Olympia.

Warris is sitting too close to me. I can feel his bony thigh rubbing against my leg, and the smell of his cheap after-shave is making me want to throw up. What the hell does Olympia see in him? He's not exactly sex on a stick.

Pippa announces to everyone that she is a famous actress.

Seriously? Who announces that kind of thing?

She follows this up with a speech about how she and Warris are teaming up for a very important movie project—a project that will blow everyone's mind. A project so huge that it will catapult her to the top of all the Latina actresses.

Is she kidding?

I think not.

March, it turns out, is a man with money who could be an investor. He's a jeweler, originally from Bolivia, who now resides in Cannes. Pippa has her eyes set firmly on his pocketbook.

"Warris is like my brother," Pippa purrs, making sure that March doesn't think she's sleeping with Warris. "We are pure soul mates," she adds, just in case he doesn't get it.

Idly I wonder what kind of name March is, and where he and Pippa met. Are they old friends? Or did she latch on to him the moment she spotted the Rolls?

I kind of figure the Rolls did it.

Soon we are crowding into a cavernlike club—the Vieux

Colombier—where musicians are up on a small stage playing live jazz, and a ton of people are gyrating on the spacious dance floor.

March's friends turn out to be three underdressed blondes and another older man with a beard, a bald head, and probably plenty of money.

Lovely! If Gino could only see me now!

Pippa and Warris slip into a double act of trying to charm the crap out of everyone, or should I say con, 'cause I've already figured out that's what they are—a couple of con artists on the prowl.

Ah, Gino would be so proud of me. I have his eye, I can spot a phony a mile away.

I wish that my father could see the potential in me. School has taught me absolutely nothing—I need to be out in the real world working next to him. Gino should be grooming me to take over his business one day, not trying to force me to stay in school. I can do it. And one day I *will* do it. Surely he must realize that there is no stopping me?

Olympia is not thrilled with the extra blondes—she is used to being front and center, and these three seasoned girls are not to her liking. Two of them are Swedish, and one is English. They are in their twenties and they are busily draping themselves all over the bald man and March.

Pippa doesn't appreciate the action. She flashes her expressive eyes before grabbing March and whisking him onto the dance floor away from temptation.

Olympia mutters "hookers" under her breath.

Unfortunately the English girl hears and fixes her with a baleful glare. "What's *your* problem, luvvie?" she questions belligerently.

Olympia backs down for once—the pot is making her mellower than usual. "No problem," she murmurs quietly. "Wanna dance?"

And there we have it. Is Olympia turning lezzie before my very eyes?

I can't believe it as the two of them head for the dance floor arm in arm, a mass of blonde hair and big boobs, all over each other.

The bald man salivates as he imagines what might happen later.

Not!

I am hardly in the blonde-with-big-boobs category—me with my wild mass of jet curls, dark eyes, and olive skin. I have my own look, thank goodness. Jon called me beautiful, that's all I need to feed my ego.

Thinking of Jon, I wonder where he is and what he's doing. Working hard as a waiter, I presume. Making money to see him through the summer.

I think I like him more than I should, even though physically he's not my type. He's too scrappy, too short, too cute.

This gets me thinking about types. Do we all have one?

Well, I know I do. Marco. Tall, dark, and handsome, what a cliché!

Where are you, Marco? What are you doing?

And then I start thinking about home and L.A. and my younger brother, Dario. How is he managing without me around? He must miss me like crazy. I am forced to admit that I have neglected him and suddenly I'm suffused with guilt. I need to contact him, tell him that I still love him and that I'll always be there for him.

But how can I do that? I'm on the run, an ocean away.

Oh crap, when Gino tracks me down—and I know that day is inevitable—there will be consequences, enormous ones.

"Let's dance," Warris says, unexpectedly grabbing my arm.

Me and Warris on the dance floor together. No *thankyouverymuch*. But Warris has had it with watching the blondes put their moves on the bald man, so I am his only option.

We hit the dance floor together just in time to see Pippa tongue Mr. Holtz's ear like she was giving him an unexpected ear job.

I can't help giggling. Is this the way she expects to raise money? Or at least raise something . . .

Warris scowls, then decides to ignore Pippa and concentrate on me. "Where you from, Lucky?" he asks, and I realize it's the first time he's called me by my name.

"L.A.," I mutter, having no desire to make conversation with Mister Sleazy.

"L.A. My kinda town," Warris says, raising his voice to be heard over the loud jazz music. "A place I'm very familiar with. I was a child star, y'know."

Yes, I do know, 'cause you've mentioned it several times.

"Really?" I try to sound as if I'm even remotely interested, which I'm not.

And because he wants me on his side, he adds—"I'm not sleeping with Pippa. You can tell that to Olympia. In fact you should."

Should I now? I don't think so, because I don't believe him. Besides, it's Olympia's problem, not mine. If she wants to keep this annoying dude around, then that's her deal.

Warris's moves on the dance floor are ridiculous, so after a few minutes I make my escape and scope out more of the crowded club.

And who do I find busying himself behind the bar? Jon.

"What're *you* doing here?" I exclaim in surprise.

"More like what are *you* doing here?" he counters.

And of course I can see that he's working as a barman, mixing drinks and handing them out.

"This is my nighttime job," he says, throwing me one of his cheeky crooked grins. "Three nights a week. Major tips."

"You didn't tell me," I say, immediately realizing how dumb I sound. After all, I've only known him for a day— why *would* I know?

"Who're you here with?" he asks.

"Old people," I reply, keeping it vague. "Friends of Olympia's."

Earlier I'd told him about my rich schoolfriend, Olympia, and that we were staying at her aunt's villa. No mention of our ages or that we are runaways. Didn't want to put him off, and if he knew I was only fifteen I'm sure he'd back away like an express train on a collision course with a juggernaut.

"Sorry I can't spend time with you," Jon says, juggling a couple of martini glasses, which are whisked out of his hands by a waitress type in a skimpy leather dress. "Thanks, Marlene," he says.

Marlene scowls at me. I scowl back.

"Take no notice of her," Jon says as Marlene vanishes into the depths of the club with the drinks. "She hates everyone, especially Americans."

"Nice," I mutter.

A man pushes past me and demands three beers and a vodka on the rocks.

I can see Jon is busy, so I decide to play it cool and return to my cozy group of misfits.

"Okay," I say, kind of reluctantly. "Then I guess I'll see you tomorrow."

"You got it," Jon says.

And that is that.

CHAPTER TWENTY-ONE

Gino Santangelo was burning up with a deep-seated dark
fury. His daughter, Lucky, had been on the missing list
for several days and he had no idea where she could be.
Costa had received the bad news from the school, whereupon Gino had immediately gotten on a plane, and with
Costa in tow, gone straight to the school in Connecticut
and interrogated the headmistress. The woman was as
furious as they were—losing a student was not the right
image to project for an exclusive private school's reputation. The headmistress suggested they call the police. Gino
responded with a flat no; he wanted no outside interfer-
ence. Instead he insisted on questioning the girls in Lucky's
class and found out absolutely nothing. Then, after getting
nowhere, he remembered the friend she'd spent the previous summer with, Olympia Stanislopoulos, and he
contacted her mother in London, who assured him that

Olympia was at the family residence in Paris taking a Russian language course.

"Double-check on her," Gino insisted.

"I don't have to," Mrs. Stanislopoulos responded in a frosty voice. "My daughter is a good girl."

Screw good girls, Gino thought. Where the hell is *my* good girl—*not*—because he was well aware that Lucky was a wild one, she always had been. He'd never been able to totally control her—she was always giving him lip, answering back, informing him that she wanted to work in the family business next to him.

Doing *what*, for chrissake? Didn't she get it? She was a girl, and girls got married, stayed home, and raised a family.

Oh yeah, right, so she didn't have a mother. But he'd always made sure to have a female presence in the house—tutors, housekeepers, and then there was Costa's wife, Jen. Lucky loved Jen, she was like a second mother to her.

Son of a bitch! Where *was* his errant daughter?

His imagination began running riot. Had she been kidnapped? Raped? Tortured? Held captive by one of his many enemies?

So many business rivals. So much shit to deal with.

He pictured Lucky tied up and alone. He had visions of her hitching a ride to California, clad in her tight faded jeans and clinging T-shirt. He imagined some asshole of a truck driver stopping to pick her up. Then he imagined the struggle, the rape, and finally his precious daughter's body being tossed from the truck.

His anger knew no bounds. He holed up in his New York apartment with Jen and Costa for company. "Lucky's a smart girl, she can look after herself," Jen kept on assuring him. "She's just like you, Gino, she'll turn up, safe and sound."

Fine for her to say. What did she know?

He called Dario at his boarding school and informed him what was going on.

Dario sounded shocked. "Sorry, Dad . . . uh, Gino . . . haven't heard from her."

"You're sure?" Gino insisted. He knew the two of them were tight and that Dario would do anything to protect his sister.

"Not a word," Dario replied.

"Listen to me, kid, if you *do* hear anything—"

"I'll call you," Dario gulped. His father always made him nervous.

Gino put down the phone and began pacing across his living room. Dario was a well-behaved kid, unlike his much wilder sister, Lucky, who seemed to think she could get away with anything. The trouble with Lucky was that she did things her way, and it wasn't right. She was only fifteen. *Fifteen*, for chrissake. A baby.

Gino shuddered at the thought of the things that could happen to her. She was unworldly. An innocent out and about in the real world. She was not street-smart or experienced. How could he protect her when he didn't even know where she was?

He contacted the Stanislopoulos girl's mother again.

"Didya check on your kid?" he demanded.

"I'm traveling, Mr. Santangelo," she answered coldly. "I'll have my assistant get back to you."

Uptight bitch! She was about as much help as a nun at a whores' convention.

"Get me the father!" he yelled at Costa, who jumped to it. "Maybe he'll be more help."

CHAPTER TWENTY-TWO

By the time we arrive back in Cannes, Olympia is in a party mood and proceeds to invite everyone up to the villa. *Really, Olympia? Why?*

In my mind I am already plotting my escape, because if Warris and his friends are moving in I have no desire to stay around.

I decide to give it another couple of days before I phone Aunt Jen and tell her that I've made a huge mistake and can she please help me get home. She'll do it, she'll do anything for me. Then of course I'll have to face Gino's wrath.

Hmm . . . I have a choice—Gino's wrath or endless time spent with a stoned Olympia and her sleazy boyfriend. Some choice.

Yes, I'm definitely moving on, unless something more than a quick crush develops with Jon. He looked quite hot behind the bar tonight. Maybe I should take it a step further than "almost."

Then again, maybe not. The thought of getting pregnant is a major deterrent. I am not *that* foolish.

Back at the villa everyone is busy getting stoned except me. I sneak off to bed and lock my door. Once again, this is not the adventure I'd hoped for.

~ ~ ~

Morning dawns and the sun is shining. It is a beautiful balmy day and I am the only one up. Apparently Pippa has stayed over, for her jacket is draped next to her purse on a chair in the living room. I wonder about March—is he here, too?

Apparently not, for the Rolls has gone, and Warris must have reclaimed the Mercedes, because it sits in the driveway.

I feel so alone; it's not a great feeling. I'm missing L.A. and Dario and the house we live in. And yes—full disclosure—I miss Marco like crazy, even if he is inclined to ignore me.

Going home does not mean I'm returning to school. No way. School is definitely over for me, and Gino better realize that he can't force me, 'cause if he does, I'll just take off again. I am ready for battle. No more school for me.

Olympia, Warris, and Pippa emerge as a happy threesome around noon. This is getting to be a routine—the noontime wake-up call. What exactly does Olympia think I do all morning? The truth of the matter is that she doesn't care. Now that she has Warris, I am totally disposable.

I am kind of disgusted by this latest turn of events. A threesome. *Really?*

Pippa looks a sight, with smeared makeup and tangled hair. She is wearing one of Warris's T-shirts, and nothing much else. Whatever happened to March? Surely he's the one they should be sleeping with since he's the one with the money to invest in their big-time movie?

"Morning, little Lucky Saint," Olympia trills, heading for the kitchen.

Oh great, now she's talking down to me. Using my fake surname like I'm some sort of dumb kid.

Pippa throws me an interested look. "Lucky Saint?" she questions. "That's a strange name."

Oh, like Pippa isn't?

"Actually it's Lucky Santangelo," I answer boldly.

"Oh my God!" Pippa exclaims, her penciled eyebrows shooting up. "Are you Gino's kid?"

What? She knows Gino? This is impossible. Did Olympia tell her?

Warris is suddenly all ears. "*The* Gino Santangelo?" he questions. "The dude who practically owns Vegas?"

There follows a long silence while I consider what I am supposed to say. Do I admit who I am? Or do I try to fake it?

Can't fake it. Not with Olympia and her big mouth.

"Yes," I say vaguely. "Breakfast, anyone?"

~ ~ ~

It is now two o'clock and I'm waiting for Jon to show, praying that he'll turn up soon, because since Warris and Pippa have discovered my identity they have been fawning all over me. It's major creepy.

I am sitting by the pool with Pippa.

"Do you know that I was engaged to one of Gino's dearest friends?" she reveals after a while, creeping me out even more.

How is this possible? Who is she?

"You were?" I mumble. "And who would that be?"

"Jake," Pippa answers proudly. "It was a long time ago—Jake the Boy, as he was known then. I was very young, but I remember the day you were born. We sent over a present—a solid gold brush and comb set with your name inscribed."

Oh crap! I know what she's talking about. There is a tarnished gold brush and comb set sitting in a box of junk Gino keeps in the basement, and it has my name engraved on the back of the brush! This box is filled with stuff nobody wants—Gino keeps it because he says some things have sentimental value.

I am in shock. How did this happen? How does a fiery Latina actress on the make know who I am?

"Where *is* Gino?" Pippa asks. "I would love to see him again."

I bet you would. Who are you?

"Gino's not here," I say, my words tumbling over each other.

"Is he coming?" Pippa asks.

I stare at her. Shortly she'll figure out how old I am and maybe wonder what's going on.

"Uh . . . yes," I lie. "He'll be here soon."

Pippa's eyes light up. "Wonderful," she purrs. "I can't wait to catch up on old times."

This is a nightmare. What to do? I have to warn Olympia, who is currently naked in the swimming pool, smoking a joint and cavorting with Warris.

I get up and hurry into the kitchen.

"So . . ." Pippa says, following me, "whose house is this?"

"It belongs to Olympia's family," I reply, wishing the woman would leave me alone.

"And they allow you two girls to live here by yourself?"

Get lost, lady. Who are you to interrogate me?

"Uh . . . yeah. Everyone will be here in a few days."

"Not a moment too soon," Pippa remarks dryly, extracting a cigarette from her purse while glancing out the window and observing Warris and Olympia in the pool.

"How old is your friend?" she asks, tapping her manicured nails on the counter.

"Nineteen," I lie, casually taking a Coca-Cola from the fridge.

"Really," Pippa says. A long pause. "And you?" she adds.

I decide a switch of subjects is in order. "You're so pretty," I say. "How old are *you*?"

This is not a question she cares to answer. I sense that age is a sensitive subject for an actress who is obviously pushing forty.

We both go outside.

"Warris," Pippa calls out. "It's time for you to drive me into town. I need to change clothes, and March is meeting us for an early drink to discuss our script."

Reluctantly, Warris hauls himself out of the pool. His shorts slip, revealing far too much of his pale anatomy. *Ugh!*

"Should I come with you?" Olympia squeaks.

"No, doll," Warris says, bending over the side of the pool to give her a kiss. "I'll be back before you know it."

Ten minutes later the terrible two are gone.

Ah, this is my opportunity to discuss the situation with Olympia. However, just as I'm about to do so, the doorbell rings, and standing on the doorstep is Jon. Cute, chirpy Jon with his crooked grin and crazy sticking-up hair. He has arrived on a Vespa, which sits in the driveway.

"Hey you," he says.

"Hey *you*," I respond, unexpectedly feeling a tad shy.

"This is quite a place."

"You found it okay," I say, stating the obvious.

"You inviting me in or am I just gonna stand here?" he asks.

"Uh . . . of course," I reply, moving back for him to enter, while hoping that Olympia has put some clothes on.

No such luck. Olympia appears in all her blonde glory, plants her legs apart, and puts her hands on her hips. "Well, hello," she says in what she considers her best sexy voice. "Who're *you*?"

"Didn't realize it was clothes optional," Jon jokes, keeping his eyes above C-level.

I am mortified. Whatever happened to the girl I used to know?

"Feel free to strip off," Olympia says, going for a major flirt. "You're hot!"

"This is my friend Jon," I say stiffly. "And nobody's stripping off."

Olympia pulls a face. "Spoilsport," she says, throwing him a knowing wink.

I quickly take his arm and steer him outside. "Sorry about that," I mumble. "Olympia dances to her own tune."

"Doesn't bother me," Jon says. "Naked blondes are not my thing."

"No?"

"No. I like 'em dark-haired and beautiful. Know who I'm talking about?"

Jon definitely has a way with words.

~ ~ ~

By the time Warris and Pippa return to the house it's dark outside, and Jon and I are locked in my room practicing "almost."

Amazing the things you can do without going all the way.

I am happy, content. I am finally having fun, and I don't give a flying anything about what the others are up to.

I may stay in the South of France longer than I thought.

CHAPTER TWENTY-THREE

Gino tracked Dimitri Stanislopoulos down by phone in Athens and asked the question—was Olympia still in Paris? Dimitri said of course she was—however, he would double-check as a courtesy.

By the time he got back to Gino he was as concerned and angry as Gino himself.

"We have a problem," Dimitri said, his voice grim.

Suddenly it was we.

"What's happening?" Gino demanded. "Have you found 'em? Are they together?"

"I'm afraid I don't know," Dimitri replied. "Olympia has apparently left Paris, taken her mother's Mercedes, and nobody knows where she's gone."

"Ahh . . ." Gino said, feeling somewhat relieved that at least Lucky was probably with her friend.

"Olympia is a very strong-minded girl," Dimitri said.

"Uncontrollable, some would say. And easily influenced. I expect that together with your daughter, Lucky . . ."

"Are you sayin' that Lucky influenced her?" Gino growled, knowing it was quite possible.

"Who knows *what* they're getting up to," Dimitri replied.

"You have any clue where they could've gone?" Gino demanded.

"No. However, I have a search out on the car. My people will soon find them."

"If your wife hadn't been so insistent about Olympia being in Paris . . ." Gino grumbled.

"*Ex*-wife," Dimitri said. "I am sure you understand how that is."

"Yes," Gino said. "I understand perfectly."

"We should meet in Paris," Dimitri said. "They can't have gone too far."

"I'll be on the next plane," Gino said.

And indeed he was.

~ ~ ~

Dimitri Stanislopoulos was not the kind of man Gino usually spent time with. He was more of an equal, and Gino was used to an entourage—men who looked up to him and hung on to his every word. After all, he was Gino Santangelo, king of the heap.

Dimitri was king of another kind of heap. A billionaire

ship owner, he lived a life of pure luxury surrounded by beautiful women and anxious yes men.

They were not so different really. Two men powerful in their own particular way. Two men who were catnip to women. Gino built magnificent hotels and gambling casinos in Vegas—among other things. And Dimitri controlled his massive empire. Apparently neither of them could control their teenage daughters.

They met up in Paris, shook hands, and went straight to Dimitri's apartment to speak with his housekeeper, Magda, a rat-faced surly woman, nervous about losing her job.

Dimitri conversed with her in rapid French, his arms flailing around like windmills.

Magda replied in a resentful mumble, pushing wisps of dyed orange hair out of her eyes.

"What did she say?" Gino wanted to know.

"She tells me that Olympia took the car last Monday— said she was going to visit her mother," Dimitri answered gruffly.

"Was Lucky with her?"

"I expect it was Lucky—apparently she was meeting a friend at the airport. Magda heard her on the phone checking arrival times."

Gino nodded. "Now how the hell do we find 'em?" he demanded impatiently.

Dimitri shrugged. "Two pretty young girls in a white convertible Mercedes. Not so hard to trace. My team is on it. They'll track the car, and Olympia's credit card charges, then we'll know where they are, or at least where they're headed."

"That easy, huh?" Gino said, chewing on his lower lip.

"Everything's easy when you set your mind to it," Dimitri said calmly.

Gino decided there was a distinct possibility that under different circumstances he and Dimitri might be friends.

After all, Gino had a great admiration for a man who could get things done.

CHAPTER TWENTY-FOUR

"There's a mistral coming," Jon informs me when he wakes up. I lean over and touch his face. He has soulful eyes and a stubbly chin. He's made me very happy. And, even better—he's not forced me to do anything I don't want to do. I think he's kind of perfect.

"What's a mistral?" I ask, stretching lazily.

"It's a vicious wind that'll knock you sideways," Jon explains, sitting up. "You should stay inside today."

"Are you kidding?" I say brightly. "It's a gorgeous day."

"Trust me," Jon warns. "It's not gonna last, and there's a storm coming through, too."

"What're you?" I joke. "A weather expert?"

"Kinda," Jon says, getting out of bed and pulling on his pants.

I am feeling euphoric. Last night spooning close to Jon, I think I might've experienced the big O everyone's always talking about. As I squeezed myself against him I suddenly felt this powerful surge of adrenaline and delight. A shudder of deliciousness took over my entire body, accompanied by a moment of pure ecstasy.

So much for not going all the way—apparently you can get all the way there without actually doing *it*.

I grin to myself and decide that Jon is a keeper.

"Will I see you later?" I ask. To my annoyance I'm beginning to sound a touch needy.

"Not today," Jon says, reaching for his shirt. "Gotta work at the café all day. Vieux Columbier all night. Tomorrow—definitely."

"What time tomorrow?" *Oh my God! Stop sounding like a clinging wimp, Santangelo. Snap out of it.*

"I'll probably make it over in the afternoon," Jon says.

"Great," I respond.

I'm feeling a bit light-headed. Does this mean I'm falling in like?

No. Too soon.

Or is it?

After declining my offer of making him breakfast, Jon heads outside, jumps on his Vespa, and zooms off.

I wander into the kitchen. Surprise, surprise, Warris and Pippa are both up.

What kind of people are they, sponging off a couple of teenage girls? I bet if Warris knew Olympia was only sixteen he'd crap himself. And surely Pippa must've figured out how old I am? But I guess math isn't her strong suit.

"Boyfriend's taken off, I see," Warris remarks, sitting at

the kitchen table chugging a mug of coffee. "Not very social, is he?"

"Jon has to work," I say, adding a pointed "Unlike *some* people."

"We're thinking of throwin' a party tonight," Warris informs me.

"Does Olympia know?" I ask.

Warris can see I'm not thrilled at the prospect of a party, but he doesn't much care what I think. Why should he? I'm only the friend.

"She knows," he says. "It's a smart business move. We'll get some big-ass money men up here, mix 'em up with a movie star or two—that's a plan that always works."

"Marabelle Blue?" I say with a hint of sarcasm.

"Is she in town?" Warris asks, suddenly looking all interested.

"No she's not," Pippa says, joining in. "She's filming in Rio. My family is thrilled—my brother even got her autograph."

"How nice," I say, and I'm dying to add, *Ha! My father got more than her autograph.* Only why give them the pleasure of knowing anything about me and my family?

By the time Olympia gets up, plans have been made. Pippa has put herself in charge. She informs us that she will take the Mercedes, drive down to Cannes, and organize everything. The right mix of guests, incredible flowers, fantastic music, delicious food. "Nobody plans a party better than Pippa," she boasts, licking her lips. "March will pay. March will do anything for me. You guys can just re-lax, I'll see you later."

And so she takes off in the Mercedes, and I go outside, dive into the pool, and begin swimming lengths. It seems like the only way to pass the day.

Idly I make up my mind that when Pippa returns I will ditch the party and drive into Juan-les-Pins. It doesn't matter that Jon will be working behind the bar—at least I can hang with him, and that sure beats sitting around with a houseful of rich, famous old people at some dumb party.

I wonder where Jon lives. I don't care if it's just one room somewhere; I think I want to move in with him if he'll have me, and why wouldn't he?

Hmm . . . I'm excited at the thought.

Olympia is hovering poolside. "Get out of the pool," she squeals. "We need to talk."

"Not if you're stoned," I respond.

"What?" Olympia says, as if she doesn't know what I'm talking about.

"Lately you're always stoned," I point out. "Warris has got you on a diet of weed, and let me tell you—it's made you major boring."

"Thanks a lot," Olympia huffs. "Maybe you're jealous 'cause *I've* got a boyfriend."

"So've I," I shoot back.

"Ha!" Olympia says. "That kid who was over here yes-terday?"

"That *kid* is way older than both of us," I say, getting out of the pool and grabbing a towel.

"I prefer me a real man," Olympia sniffs. "Someone who can *teach* me something."

"You're so full of it," I fume. She's really annoying, and it infuriates me that she's only decided to speak to me because Warris isn't around, he's busy taking an afternoon nap. "Y'know," I say, thinking it's about time I tell her how I feel. "Lately you've been acting like a real bitch."

Olympia tosses back her blonde hair and glares at me, her blue eyes full of spite. "You're still such a baby," she sneers. "You simply don't get it."

"Oh, I get it all right," I retaliate. "Some random dude comes along, and that's it for our friendship. Why have a best friend when a guy'll do so much better?"

"That's not true."

"Take a look at yourself, it's totally true. This was supposed to be *our* adventure. Not joined at the hip with sleazy Warris and his would-be movie-star girlfriend."

"Pippa is so *not* his girlfriend."

"Then what were the three of you doing in bed together?" I demand. "Playing tennis?"

"God!" Olympia exclaims. "You're such a little prude."

"No, I'm not," I argue. "I'm smart, a lot smarter than you. I can see through people. Warris is a user and you should open your eyes, 'cause he's using you big-time."

Before Olympia can answer, it starts to rain, a light rain at first, but as it gets heavier we both make a dash inside.

I turn to face Olympia. "I'm thinking of leaving," I say.

"Go ahead," Olympia snaps, not even one bit concerned. "If you're so bloody miserable it's probably for the best."

And with that she stalks off to the master bedroom to join her lover, leaving me to plan my next move.

Yes, once Pippa gets back with the car, I am definitely taking it and driving to Juan-les-Pins to hang out with Jon. He can help me decide what to do, and hopefully he'll suggest that I move in with him.

Sounds like the perfect plan.

CHAPTER TWENTY-FIVE

Once Dimitri received word of Olympia's credit card purchases, leaving a trail from Paris to the South of France—mostly at gas stations and convenience stores—he and Gino headed for the airport and a private plane. Dimitri had a hunch he knew exactly where they'd be: He figured they'd hide out at his sister's house above Cannes—Olympia had always loved it there. The advantage of owning your own plane is that it is on call anytime you need it, so Dimitri always had his on standby. Why not? He was never sure when he would feel like taking off and going somewhere. Rome, Venice, New York, London. Best to be prepared. Dimitri was a man who enjoyed acting on a whim.

Tracking down teenagers was not exactly the whim he had in mind, but it seemed that it had to be done.

Gino, on the other hand, preferred things organized. He had not planned on flying to Europe on a wild chase to track down Lucky. This trip was out of his comfort zone, and he realized that he should've brought Costa with him—he was annoyed that he hadn't. Costa, along with his wife, Jen, was always the voice of reason, the calming influence. They were family—the family Gino had never had. Ah yes, once there had been the beautiful Maria, the wife he'd cherished and adored, the mother of his children, the keeper of his heart. However, Maria had been taken from him in such a vile and brutal way. A way he would never forget.

He still mourned her death; he had not yet learned to celebrate her life.

Now Lucky had put this stress on him. He didn't need it. He didn't need to be traveling halfway across the world for the *second* time, to bring home his child. Lucky might think she was all grown up, but the truth was she was still just a child, with no thought of the consequences of her behavior. Damn her! He was furious, yet at the same time relieved that she was with a friend and not running around on her own.

The two men sipped large tumblers of scotch while they discussed the difficulties of raising daughters without a permanent female presence. It was the one thing that they both had in common.

"My ex-wife doesn't seem to care *what* Olympia gets up to," Dimitri complained. "She's too busy roaming the world in search of the latest beauty treatments, or some transient stud willing to spend my money."

Gino nodded. He understood. Of all the girlfriends he'd had come and go since Maria's untimely death, none of them had been remotely interested in bonding with his daughter. He'd relied on housekeepers and private tutors— and possibly that was his mistake, for now he had a wild child on his hands, a girl who obviously had no intention of staying in school.

"Lucky is very willful," Gino said. "She didn't used to be, but since I sent her away to boarding school . . ." He trailed off. Was Lucky acting out because she thought he'd abandoned her?

No.

Maybe?

Perhaps he should have been paying more attention to her.

"Here's what we should do," Dimitri said, only half joking. "Marry them off. Make them somebody else's problem."

Gino nodded again. Not a bad idea. Why hadn't he thought of it? Maybe *that* was exactly what Lucky needed. An arranged marriage. It wasn't such a bizarre idea at all.

Shortly before landing, Dimitri received a message that turned his craggy features ashen.

Gino sensed trouble. "What's the problem?" he demanded.

Dimitri spoke in low tones. "My people have tracked the Mercedes," he said. "It was involved in an accident.

The car is a write-off. And behind the wheel the police found the body of an unidentified female."

Gino felt his world collapse around him.

Was the female Lucky?

Was his daughter dead?

CHAPTER TWENTY-SIX

It's almost five o'clock and no Pippa, although what we do have is a downpour of nonstop rain and howling winds. It seems as if the entire house is rattling. I've already packed my bag in anticipation of Pippa's return. Quite frankly, I can't wait to get out of here. Olympia and Warris are running around the house removing the few remaining dust-sheets covering the furniture and preparing for a party. I can't stand either of them, and I'm certainly not about to help. It's not *my* party.

I can hear Warris complaining about Pippa. "That woman is always late," he bitches. "Knowing Pippa, she'll probably turn up with everything a few minutes before the guests."

"Do we know who the guests are?" Olympia asks, hopeful that among them there will be a movie star or two. Olympia is a bit of a fame groupie.

"People with money," Warris replies confidently. "Big-time investors." He pauses for a moment—then—"You can tell 'em who your father is, it won't hurt for them to know you're a Stanislopoulos. And you gotta flirt a bit, keep 'em happy."

What a pimp! I hate him more every day.

"Help me choose what to wear," Olympia pleads, oblivious to the fact that she's living with a snake.

"Something low cut and sexy," Warris replies. "Show off your tits."

She's sixteen, dude, and you're an asshole.

"You gotta sex it up, doll," Warris continues, getting into it. "You gotta get 'em all excited."

And with those words ringing in the air, the two of them zoom off to raid her aunt's closet.

I realize that Olympia is totally clueless when it comes to Warris, and unfortunately there's absolutely nothing I can do about it.

~ ~ ~

Time passes. The rain gets stronger, so does the wind. Darkness creeps in and it's now almost seven o'clock.

No Pippa. No Mercedes. No food, music, or incredible flowers. No party.

I can hear Warris and Olympia arguing. I shut the door to my room and wait.

Where *is* Pippa, party-planner supreme? Where's the

freaking car so that I can get out of here? Why have I allowed myself to get trapped like this?

I am mad at myself for doing so, but how was I to know that Olympia would turn out to be so selfish?

I wish I was older. I wish I had my own money, or at least a credit card like Olympia. When I'd asked Gino, he'd informed me that I didn't need one.

Why not, Daddy Dearest? Why the hell not?

I'm worried about pushing myself on Jon with nothing to support myself with.

Hmm . . . maybe I can be a waitress at the café Jon works at; I'm sure he can swing it so they hire me. Now that would be one cool trip, working together side by side. I like it!

Lucky Santangelo. Waitress.

Not quite the start I'd envisioned for myself, but I guess it will have to do for now.

CHAPTER TWENTY-SEVEN

Once they landed at Nice Airport, Dimitri and Gino immediately transferred to a private helicopter. Gino wasn't fond of helicopters, especially in such foul weather. The wind was roaring and the rain teeming down, but he boarded anyway. It wouldn't do to appear weak in front of Dimitri, and besides, he was desperate to find out who the female body in the car was. Olympia or Lucky? Jesus Christ. He broke out in a cold sweat just thinking about it. If it was Lucky, he would never forgive himself. Since Maria's murder he'd been so careful to make sure she was protected at all times. Obviously he'd failed. He recalled the last time he'd seen his daughter—it was at the New York apartment, an awkward dinner for two. Lucky had protested about being sent off to another school, but what was he supposed to do? She needed discipline, so boarding school it was. He was only doing what he thought was best for her.

The following morning Lucky had been picked up by limo and spirited off to her new school in Connecticut. He hadn't gone with her. He was still mad about Switzerland and her bedtime adventure with some nameless boy. She was fifteen years old, for chrissake. Her behavior was out of control.

Now he regretted his coldness. Surely he should've spent more time with her, tried to discover the reason she was rebelling?

Too late now. Too damn late.

~ ~ ~

After the helicopter landed in Cannes, a car drove Gino and Dimitri directly to the morgue. Both men entered with heavy hearts, dreading what they might find. They were met by two French detectives and a morgue assistant who escorted them to a room where they were asked to identify the body.

Gino attempted to remain calm. If the body from the car was Lucky, would he ever get over it?

No. Never.

And if the body was Olympia, then where was Lucky?

CHAPTER TWENTY-EIGHT

This is beyond ridiculous. I am so fed up and at a loss as to what to do next. Warris and Olympia have given up on all thoughts of a party and returned to the master bedroom, where I can clearly hear them getting it on. Squeals and grunts and the occasional "Oh *yeees*, more please!" Is there anything worse than listening to other people making out? I think not.

It's quite obvious that Pippa has absconded with the Mercedes and has no intention of ever returning. Which means I am stuck, well and truly stuck.

I am totally pissed off until suddenly—like a miracle—I see the lights of a car approaching up the driveway, and I am filled with relief. Pippa is back, and I'm getting the hell out of here.

Jon, I'm on my way!

Grabbing my packed bag, I make a run for the door and

race outside. The rain pours relentlessly down. I don't care, I just want out.

The car approaches, and I stare into the murky darkness, realizing that it's not the Mercedes, it's a black sedan, and it's pulling up in front of the house.

By this time I am totally drenched as I hover on the doorstep like a half-drowned rat. But nothing will stop me now, because freedom beckons, and whoever's in the car can definitely give me a ride. I'm determined.

And then—oh my God!

Gino emerges from the car followed by Olympia's dad, and I am in a state of total panic.

Gino takes one look at me, then grabs me by the shoulders, his nails digging into my flesh, before he starts shaking me so hard that I think I might throw up.

"You stupid dumb fuckin' *kid*!" he screams in true Gino style. "You dumbass *idiot*."

While Dimitri crows a triumphant "I knew it! I knew they'd be here," Gino shoves me back into the house, and Dimitri follows.

My mind zips into overdrive. How do I warn Olympia that the fathers are here? How do I get her out of bed with Mister Slime? I realize we're not the best of friends at the moment, but this is a huge big deal and I should try to help her.

Gino is glaring at me balefully, while Dimitri is looking around at the chaos and muttering, "My *God*! They've wrecked my sister's house."

Gino grabs me again while I send an urgent silent message to Olympia: *Put on some clothes and get out of the bedroom.*

Too late. Dimitri is on a rampage searching for his daughter. He flings open the double doors of the main bedroom and there is Olympia—naked of course—on her knees servicing Warris.

Dimitri does not hesitate; he moves forward and whacks her across her exposed ass with all his might.

Olympia shrieks.

Dimitri screams, "Christ!"

And Warris falls off the bed.

I realize that my life as I know it is over.

~ ~ ~

Later we learn about Pippa. It's a huge shock, especially for Warris, who is attempting to pack his bags because Dimitri has ordered him to get the hell out of his house immediately before he summons the police and has him arrested for trespassing.

"What'm I supposed to do?" Warris whines to Olympia. "I got no car, how'm I supposed to get down to Cannes? It's storming out."

Dimitri overhears and fixes Warris with a grim look. "You're lucky I don't break both your legs," he snarls. "Get out of here—*now!*"

Warris doesn't need telling twice. He scoops up his bag and reluctantly slouches out into the heart of the storm.

Olympia pulls a sulky face and screws up her small eyes. "It's not like we've done anything wrong," she mutters in a complaining voice. "We were just taking a vacation."

Dimitri glares her down. He's powerful and in charge and does not wish to listen to any excuses. He turns to Gino. "We should head back to the airport," he says abruptly. "My plane is on standby."

Gino nods. "Let's go."

Dimitri looks around again, his lip curled in disgust. "This place needs fumigating," he says. "It smells like some kind of filthy pot den. My people will deal with it."

Gino agrees. He can't seem to look at me, or maybe it's me who can't look at him.

I hate him.

I think.

I guess it's on to the next chapter.

CHAPTER TWENTY-NINE

On one hand, Gino to the rescue is a good thing. At least it gets me away from the house of pot, although I would've preferred to be somewhere with Jon, who I am beginning to realize I might never see again, because an hour after Gino and Dimitri discovered where we were, the four of us are on Dimitri's plane heading for Paris. *Good-bye, South of France.*

Good-bye, waitress job.

Good-bye, me and Jon.

It's all a major shock, especially the news about Pippa. I can't believe that she's gone, it doesn't seem real.

Just for a change Gino is giving me the silent treatment. After his initial blowup he proceeds to ignore me as if I don't exist. In a way I'd rather he was yelling and screaming—at least then I'd know he cares.

Olympia is coming back to earth with a bang. No sex with sleazy Warris. No grass. No freedom. We're both busted and she knows it.

We are sitting next to each other on the plane. Neither of us are too happy.

Olympia stares at me accusingly. "Did you tell them where to find us?" she demands in a hoarse whisper. "Did you?"

I'm horrified that she would even think it was me. "No way," I answer, quite insulted. "As if I would."

"Wouldn't put it past you," she mutters.

"What?"

"Oh, don't play the innocent with me," she snarls. "I know you hated Warris."

The last thing I expected was for Olympia to blame me. We sink into an uncomfortable silence and soon we both fall asleep.

When Dimitri's plane arrives in Paris we part ways without a word. My once best friend is now my enemy.

How did *that* happen?

The answer.

Warris. Mister Sleaze.

~ ~ ~

My father and I sit in a VIP lounge waiting for a flight to New York or L.A. I'm not sure where he has in mind to take me next. He's still not talking.

I watch him as he interacts with the hostesses in the lounge who are fussing all over him because they obviously fancy him. Gino the Ram, with his dark good looks and wicked smile, he's quite a catch. And I suppose I have to admit that he *is* a very charismatic man.

After a while I ask him where we are headed.

"Home," he answers brusquely. "Where you belong."

This gets me thinking. Where *do* I belong? Apparently not in the South of France with Jon—I can write him off as a boy I'm probably never going to see again. So . . . do I belong in Gino's New York apartment? Probably not. Then we must be on our way to L.A. and the Bel Air mausoleum.

Oh great! Back to homeschooling and serious lockdown. And . . . *Marco.* Yes, the good news is that I'll be seeing Marco again, so maybe things are looking up. That's if he doesn't continue to treat me like a kid. Which I'm so not.

How do I convince him of this?

Hmm . . . gotta think about it. Gotta come up with a plan.

~ ~ ~

I am right, Bel Air it is. Lush, beautiful Bel Air, a maze of winding streets filled with mysterious gated mansions and an abundance of greenery and palm trees. Home. My home.

We arrive in the afternoon, and all I want to do is throw myself in the welcoming blue swimming pool and wash away our miserable travels.

A woman is at the door to greet us. An athletic type in a jogging suit, with mousy hair pulled back into a ponytail. She is thirtyish, not my father's type at all. "This is Miss Drew," Gino says. "She'll be keepin' an eye on you."

I should've known. Miss Drew must be my latest prison guard. Great!

"I don't need anyone to keep an eye on me," I say sulkily. "I'll be sixteen in a few weeks. I can look after myself."

"Sure you can," Gino says with a sarcastic twist. "Just like your girlfriend the whore."

Oh my God, is he actually calling Olympia a whore? *Wow!* That's major cold. Besides, if she's a whore, what does that make him? I can't keep track of all the women he's been linked with, and I certainly don't want to.

Gino the Ram or Gino the male whore?

I giggle at the thought.

Miss Drew shoots me a look.

Gino scowls and vanishes into the house.

"I'll take you up to your room," Miss Drew says.

"Excuse me?" I retort, standing tall. "This is my *home.* I don't need you taking me anywhere."

"Your father said I was to—"

"*What?*" I say, giving her a baleful glare.

She backs down.

Ha! Perhaps this is one tutor/guard/housekeeper I can control. After all, I'm not Gino's daughter for nothing.

I take off to my room and fling myself on the bed. Miss Drew chooses not to follow me. Smart woman, she knows when she's not wanted.

I start reflecting on everything that's happened. Running away from school in Connecticut; the crazy drive to the South of France; Olympia's aunt's villa; Olympia hooking up with Warris; ah, Pippa. Poor Pippa. No future stardom for her. And finally, Jon. I guess I'll never see *him* again. Too sad.

Miss Drew appears at the door to my room shortly after seven.

"Your father wishes you to join him for dinner," she says, all crisp and proper. "Seven-thirty in the dining room."

Oh yippee! I can't wait. Another silent evening of fun.

As I change my clothes for dinner I decide that whether Gino wants to talk to me or not, I am having it out with him. He needs to know how I feel. I am not his little puppet that he can control. I cannot be ignored. It's not fair, and I refuse to stand for it. Surely he must realize that by now?

When I enter the dining room, Gino is already there, sitting at the table reading a newspaper. He lowers the paper when he sees me and throws me a quizzical look. "So, kiddo," he says in quite a friendly fashion. "What are we gonna do about you?"

Relief floods through me. It seems I don't have to force anything—he's opening up a dialogue and I am thrilled.

"I'm sorry," I blurt, 'cause I'm sure that's exactly what he wants to hear.

"For what?" he retorts.

"For dragging you halfway across the world to get me."

He raises an eyebrow. "That's *all* you're sorry for?"

"Well . . . yes," I answer sheepishly, because I'm sure as crap not sorry about ditching school. Why should I be? He shouldn't've sent me there in the first place. *Bad move, Daddy.*

Gino doesn't say anything for a moment. He picks up his tumbler of Jack and Coke and takes a hearty swig. "You remind me of someone," he says at last. "Yeah, I gotta say that you really do."

"Who?" I ask.

"Me," he says, accompanied by a throaty chuckle.

I give him a long bold look. "Surely that's a good thing?"

"If you were a boy—yeah. Only you're not a boy, Lucky, you're a girl an' you gotta learn how to behave like one."

"Says who?"

"Says me."

We lock eyes. Matching eyes. Black and intense. I can feel myself becoming more like him every day, and it's not a bad thing. I *want* to have the strength that my father has. I *want* to be the female Gino. I *want* him to accept me for who I am.

"Girls can do anything a boy can do," I remind him. "Or at least this girl can."

"So stubborn," Gino says, with a heavy sigh.

"And you're not?" I respond.

"Jesus!" Gino shakes his head. "You need protectin' from yourself. You're a wild one."

"No wilder than you were when you were my age," I throw back at him.

"Once again, little lady, I'm gonna remind you that you're a girl, an' my job is t'see that you don't go gettin' into any more trouble."

How are you planning on doing that? I want to ask. Only I don't, because I sense this conversation has gone far enough for now, and I know I shouldn't push it. Cleverly I move on to another subject.

"How's Dario?" I ask.

"He's doin' fine," Gino answers. "He'll be comin' home this weekend, so you two can catch up, spend some time together."

"Is he liking his school?"

"Better than you liked yours," Gino answers dryly. "At least he's stayin' there."

"Maybe we can all do something together," I venture. "Like as a family."

"No chance, kiddo," Gino says, holding back a yawn. "Vegas calls."

"Can we come with you?" I ask boldly, knowing the answer will be no.

My father doesn't disappoint. "Sorry, kiddo," he says, like it's no big deal. "Vegas is not a place for you kids to be hangin' out."

Okay then. But one day it will be, 'cause one day I am going to take over the family business, and build my own hotels. You can bet on it, Daddy. Because I, Lucky Santangelo, am eventually going to rule!

CHAPTER THIRTY

I hug Dario tightly when he arrives back from his school. He's so freaking handsome and major tall. He could be a surfer with his longish blond hair and athletic build. It seems that while I haven't been watching, my little brother has grown up, and although not exactly a man, he's definitely on his way. It feels so amazing to see him. I keep on hugging him until he finally shoves me away.

"Quit bein' so clingy," he says gruffly.

What? Me clingy? Who's he kidding?

"Excuse *me*?" I say with a haughty shrug. "You should *be* so fortunate."

"You look better than last time I saw you," Dario says, squinting at me, his eyes so clear and blue. "What've you been up to?"

"Stuff you're too young to know about," I answer mysteriously.

Dario snorts with laughter. "I know plenty," he says.

"You're still a kid," I respond.

He cocks his head to one side. "You think?"

"I know."

"Bullcrap."

"Language!"

We both break into giggles, and for a moment I feel the unbreakable bond we've always had. It's a warm and wonderful feeling. I have a brother and he loves me and I love him back. My one and only real family connection.

"Uh . . . did Marco drive you here?" I ask, attempting to keep it casual.

Dario throws me a knowing look. "You still got a big fat crush on him?" he teases.

"What?" I say vaguely.

"You heard."

"Of course not," I say with a fierce frown.

Dario grins. "Yeah, *sure*."

"Well," I continue, determined not to crack. "Did he drive you or not?"

"He's downstairs. Why don't you go catch up before he leaves for Vegas with Dad? You know you want to."

"Marco's going to Vegas, too?"

"Yes," Dario singsongs, mimicking me, "Marco's going to Vegas, too."

Oh God, I forgot how annoying Dario can be.

"Maybe I will," I say, making a dash for the mirror to make sure I am presenting my best self. After all, Marco hasn't seen the new sophisticated me. It'll probably be lust at first sight and I'll have to fight him off.

"He's never gonna notice you as anything more than Gino's kid," Dario remarks. "You realize that, don't you?"

I favor him with a creative scowl. "You know nothing," I say.

"I know plenty," Dario replies.

"You're still a kid and I'm *so* not," I inform him.

He narrows his blue eyes. "Wanna bet?"

We lock stares. I have to admit that he certainly doesn't look like a kid anymore.

"You found yourself a girlfriend?" I ask.

"More like a boyfriend," Dario blurts.

There follows a long silence while I digest this piece of crazy information. Surely Dario isn't telling me he's gay?

Oh . . . my . . . God. It can't possibly be true. If it is, Gino will kill him. Gino could *never* accept having a gay son.

Dario is busy giving me a look that screams, *Well, aren't you going to say something?*

I am too shocked to open my mouth. It's not as if I have anything against gays—the truth is I barely know any—but Dario, my own brother. How did *that* happen?

"Have you told Dad?" I gasp, torn between being horrified and supportive.

"No freaking way," Dario replies. "And don't you *dare*."

"As if," I snort. "It's your deal, not mine." I pause for a moment, then add, "Are you sure?"

"Sure 'bout what?"

"Uh . . . being gay?"

"I hate that word."

"Well, what else would you call it?"

"How the fuck would I know?" Dario snaps, glaring at me balefully as if this is my fault.

It's all becoming a bit surreal—when I first left for boarding school Dario was a lanky teenager into cars and comics. Now he's telling me he's into other boys. Wow!

"So," I say, treading carefully. "How did this happen?"

Dario shrugs. "It didn't just happen. I think I've always known, but I was too scared to face it."

I nod understandingly. It's quite obvious that Dario has been dying to tell someone, and here I am—his big sister—the person closest to him. I am touched that he feels safe enough to confide in me.

"There's this art teacher at school," Dario continues. "His name is Eric."

I nod my head again, encouraging him to tell me everything, although I'm kind of shocked that it's a teacher he's hooking up with.

"Well . . . Eric invited me to spend the weekend at his place, 'cause he noticed I never went home on weekends. And . . . uh . . . I went there, and stuff just kinda happened."

I don't press him for details, not my business. However, I do warn him that he'd be wise to keep this information to himself. Then I hug my not so little brother, and tell him that I love him and that eventually he'll be able to come out and announce his gayness to the whole world—but not now, not while we're living under Gino's roof.

He agrees, and we hug some more, and somehow or other seeing Marco before he hotfoots it to Vegas with Gino does not seem so important.

Family first. That's my new motto. And Dario is my only true family.

CHAPTER THIRTY-ONE

Since Gino took off for Vegas, it's been extremely quiet at the Bel Air house. This suits me and Dario fine, 'cause I've kind of enjoyed bonding with my brother again. Now that I know he's not such a kid, I tell him about some of *my* adventures. He eats it up, and starts to tell *me* more about Eric—not the sex bits, more about what a nice guy Eric is, and how much he likes him. Hey—as long as my little brother is happy, I only want the best for him. Most nights we are able to dodge out of the house, escaping Miss Drew's watchful eye. We hang out in Westwood taking in a movie and scoffing pizza.

Do I miss Jon?

Not really, especially when I eyeball the amount of talent cruising Westwood, mostly students from UCLA.

Dario and I make a good team. Between us we start hanging out with various kids we meet along the way. I am in desperate need of a new crush, and just in time, along comes Scott.

Scott's black, and black is beautiful—which just about sums him up. He's tall, plays basketball, speaks three languages, and has a smile to die for.

Scott is from New York, where his parents are both lawyers. He's twenty. I inform him that I'm eighteen. We originally ran into each other at a pizza parlor and it was lust at first sight. For a couple of nights we hang out with Dario in tow, then Eric arrives in town for a visit, so Dario is off and running, leaving me and Scott to do our thing.

He takes me to a movie, and after we settle comfortably in the back row we create magic that has nothing to do with the film playing on the screen.

Wow! This is a boy with all the moves, and suddenly Jon is a very distant memory indeed, and Scott is front and center.

I can't help giggling when I think about what Gino's reaction would be to his two darling children. One gay, and one making out with a black guy. Oh yes, Gino would throw a freaking fit!

Miss Drew makes a vain attempt to keep Dario and me in check, however she soon realizes she's fighting a losing battle and pretends not to know what we're up to.

We're out every night, and I am having the best time. My only worry is—what does Gino have in store for me? He dragged me back from the South of France, plonked me down in our Bel Air house, and pissed off to Vegas—now what?

I guess I'll just have to wait and see. Meanwhile I'm enjoying every moment with Scott, although he's getting a bit impatient about my "everything but" rule. "Y'know, Lucky, you're not a kid," he informs me after one particularly heavy necking session. "You're eighteen, so what're you waiting for? You can't stay a virgin forever."

I'm waiting to be legal, I want to say. But I don't, because that would freak him out, and I've decided that Scott is a keeper. So I continue stringing him along, making sure he's always a satisfied customer—if you get my drift.

Dario is delighted to see Eric and spend time with him. So Dario and I are two happy little campers until Miss Drew informs us that Gino will be home tomorrow and we'd better curtail our out-of-the-house activities—whatever they might be.

Ah . . . she should only know.

~ ~ ~

Gino is back from Vegas and he's in an excellent mood. Apparently he has two new best friends, Senator Peter Richmond and his wife, Betty. He has invited them for dinner, and he wants me and Dario to be present at the dinner. What a major drag—neither of us is thrilled.

I encounter Marco in the hallway. He is still so

handsome—dark and brooding. For a moment I almost forget about Scott, but only for a moment.

"How are you, Marco?" I ask, wondering if he is regarding me with new eyes.

"Doin' okay," Marco says, walking away from me and heading for the kitchen.

Hmm . . . he's obviously attracted to me and doesn't care to show it.

I follow him into the kitchen. "So," I say, reaching for an apple. "How was Vegas?"

"The usual," Marco says, refusing to make eye contact.

I take a bite of apple and edge closer to him. "What does *that* mean?"

"It means that you don't wanna know what goes on in Vegas."

"Oh yes I do," I say, eager to hear whatever he has to tell me.

"Y'know somethin'," Marco says, finally looking at me. "You are some piece of work, Lucky."

"I am?"

"You am."

"And why's that?" I ask boldly.

"'Cause your act is gettin' old."

I glare at him. "Excuse me?"

"Y'know exactly what I mean. Running away to Europe. Givin' Gino a ton of crap. How about growing up for a change? Actin' like a person."

My mouth drops open in surprise. How *dare* he talk to me like that. He's an employee. I'm Gino's daughter. He has major nerve.

I decide that I hate him.

"Screw you, Marco," I spit in his direction, and before he can respond, I back out of the kitchen and make a dash for my room.

~ ~ ~

The Richmonds are middle-aged and superboring. Why Gino wants me and Dario at this dinner is beyond me.

Betty Richmond has one of those long horsey faces you see on the society pages, while Peter Richmond obviously fancies himself as a charmer. He's also a major letch, 'cause I catch him ogling my tits through my T-shirt. Obviously a pervert.

"What a pretty young lady," he remarks to Gino.

I loathe being called pretty; the very word conjures up images of a stupid blonde girl with a fixed smile and perfect teeth. That is not me at all—I like to think of my looks as edgy and unusual.

"She's smart, too," Gino says, joining in.

Huh? Compliments from Daddy Dearest? What's up with *that*?

Dario and I exchange disgusted looks. Neither of us wants to be at this dinner—unfortunately, we were given no choice.

"Lucky, dear," Betty Richmond says in a thin, tinkly voice.

"Yes?" I answer politely, noting that she has lipstick on her teeth and cold dead eyes.

"Why don't you tell me about yourself."

Again, *huh?* Is she kidding? What does she want to know?

I run over what I *could* say. Hmm . . . *my name's Lucky Santangelo; Gino saw fit to name me after a notorious Chicago gangster. When I was five I came across my mother's naked blood-drenched body floating on a raft in the family swimming pool. After that I was kind of kept locked away from the real world until I was sent off to boarding school in Switzerland, where I discovered the joy of boys. Bingo! I like nothing more than major make-out sessions and seeing how far I can take it without going all the way.*

"There's not much to tell," I answer vaguely.

Betty purses her thin lips, while Peter takes another surreptitious glance at my boobs.

"Lucky's gonna make a wonderful wife for some fortunate guy one of these days," Gino says with a friendly chuckle. "An' whoever that guy is—the little bastard gets *me* for a father-in-law. Some deal, huh?"

Talk about an inflated ego. Gino has it going on bigtime. And no, I am not making anyone a wonderful wife, I am conquering the world first, and who knows—maybe I'll *never* get married. It's my choice whatever I do.

"Of course," Betty murmurs in answer to Gino's comment.

"Do you have children?" I ask Betty, striving to be polite.

"We have a daughter and a son, Craven," Betty replies.

"Yes, and he's a handsome son of a bitch," Peter booms.

"That he is," Gino agrees. "You're gonna meet him, Lucky. We're all gettin' together in Vegas."

"When?" I venture.

"Soon enough," Gino says.

~ ~ ~

Later, Dario and I make our escape through our usual downstairs window. We've called a cab to pick us up two houses away. By eleven we're cruising Westwood. By twelve I'm shacked up with Scott at his place while his roommate is making out with a girl in the other room. Scott's got it going on, and I am seriously contemplating going all the way when there is a minor earthquake—one of the joys of living in L.A.—and I realize I'd better get back to the house before someone starts checking on me and discovers I'm missing.

Dario and I meet up at a designated spot, and Eric gives us a ride back to our house.

We enter through the downstairs window and quietly make it up to our bedrooms. Nobody is around. My bed is still filled with bolsters and pillows so it looks as if I'm asleep under the pile of covers, should anyone care.

I give a sigh of relief and collapse into bed.

Soon I'll be sixteen. It's about time I started thinking about my future.

CHAPTER THIRTY-TWO

Gino doesn't stay in L.A. for long. After dinner with the Richmonds he is preparing to take off again, this time to New York. A couple of days later he leaves with a promise that Vegas is definitely in my future. I start thinking that perhaps he's lined up a school for me in Vegas—now *that* I can deal with. Before he goes I manage to get him to agree that I can take driving lessons, and since Dario has to return to his school in San Diego I am delighted to have something to do during the day.

My driving instructor is named Carlos, a man with a devilish smile. He's Latino and short—but quite attractive in an older-man kind of way. The thing is, I can already drive, so hanging out with Carlos for a couple of hours a day is a bonus. He's funny and he sings aloud as if he's planning to be the next Marc Anthony. We get along fine. Too fine, because although he wears a thick gold wedding band it doesn't take long before he comes on to me.

What is it with men? Do they all walk around with a permanent hard-on, waiting to pounce?

I tell Carlos that I'm a virgin, and that he'd better back off or I'll inform my father. This quiets him down, but after that things are not the same, and I get Miss Drew to cancel any further lessons and to book me a driving test, which I am happy to report that I pass. Now all I have to do is wait for Gino's return, and hope that he'll surprise me with a car for my sixteenth birthday. Wouldn't *that* be something.

Meanwhile, things are not going smoothly with Scott. He's totally pushing me to go further than I'm prepared to, and we end up having a fierce fight, during which I scream at him, "I'm fifteen, you jerk!" And that's the last I've seen of Scott. I guess age *does* matter.

So how am I filling my days waiting for Gino to come home? Well, I've rediscovered reading and I've become obsessed with the biographies of well-known, successful businessmen and how they made it all the way to the top. Hey—riveting stuff. I'm totally into it.

Learning is the new me. No more stupid boys who are only after one thing.

Wow! Am I finally growing up? I think I am.

~ ~ ~

On the morning of my sixteenth birthday I awake to the news that Gino is back in L.A. Miss Drew knocks on my door and informs me that my father would love me to join him for breakfast on the patio.

I experience a tingle of excitement as I jump out of bed. Will there be a Mercedes or a Porsche waiting for me in the driveway? All shiny and new, wrapped in a great big bow? Oh *yes!*

I pull on my jeans and T-shirt and hurry downstairs.

I am sixteen. Almost an adult. No more school for me. I want to get into my father's business. I want to learn every-thing. I know I can do it.

Gino greets me with a smile and a "Happy birthday, kiddo."

A hug would've been nice, but he doesn't move from his seat at the outdoor table.

"Hi, Daddy," I say, "welcome back."

"You bin behavin' yourself?" he asks.

"Of course," I reply.

"Good t'know," he says. "'Cause I've decided to open a bank account for you. Plus I'm givin' you that credit card you're always carryin' on about. I figured it's about time you learned how to manage money."

Hmm . . . a bank account and a credit card. *Yippee.* Not quite a car, but still an excellent way to start the day.

"Wow!" I murmur. "Thanks."

"Nobody gave me nothin' when *I* hit sixteen," Gino of-fers. "But I guess—since you're my kid—I can spoil you if I feel like it. Right?"

I nod attentively and slide into a chair opposite him.

He still hasn't said a word about the South of France and that whole episode. I keep on expecting some kind of dire punishment, but nothing so far. Maybe he loves me after all, and is simply relieved to get me back in one piece.

I reach for a slice of toast and slather it with butter.

"How was New York?" I ask.

"Same old same old," Gino replies.

"Did you see Aunt Jen and Uncle Costa?"

"Sure. Had a coupla things I wanted to check out with Jen."

"What things?" I ask curiously.

"Stuff about you, if you wanna know."

"Me?" I say, quite startled.

"Yeah, you." Gino nods his head. "Does that surprise you?"

"Uh . . . I never really thought about it."

"Well, start thinkin', 'cause I think I kinda solved our problem."

"What problem?" I ask, although I know exactly what problem he's talking about. Me and school. A horrible match. I swear if he sends me to another boarding school I'll simply take off again, and this time I'll make sure he doesn't find me.

Gino shrugs and sips his coffee—black and strong. "You got a pretty dress?" he inquires.

Shows how well he knows me. I hate wearing dresses—not my style at all.

"Why?" I ask carefully.

"'Cause we're goin' to Vegas exactly like I promised."

"We are?" I ask, suddenly major excited. "When?"

"Today, kiddo. Gotta celebrate your birthday in style, an' tonight there's this big charity event I'm hosting for Betty Richmond at my hotel, so go pack somethin' nice—I don't wanna see you in those crummy jeans an' T-shirt. You're my kid, you gotta shine."

Really? I'm his kid, am I? And the party I'm going to in Las Vegas is not for me, it's for uptight Betty Richmond— our lady of the cold dead eyes.

I am half furious, but only half, because at least I get to go to Vegas, and I guess that's a bonus I can live with.

CHAPTER THIRTY-THREE

Las Vegas is one big major thrill! Bright lights, sidewalks teeming with people, a mass of frantic activity. Everything is so unlike the staid winding streets of Bel Air. And as for the towering neon-lit hotels, all I can say is—wow! I'm excited. I can't wait to get out of the limo driving us from the airport and explore the streets. However, no such luck, because the limo deposits me and Gino at his latest hotel, and I am whisked up to his penthouse suite where I am to stay. Gino immediately takes off, leaving me in the charge of Flora, a thirty-something woman with a fixed smile, dyed red hair, and obvious fake boobs. She is one of the VIP hostesses at the hotel, and has obviously received a full set of instructions from Gino about where she is supposed to take me, and what we are supposed to do.

I am pissed. Where is my freedom? Why is there always someone around to watch over me like I'm some kind of crazed criminal? *Leave me alone, people!*

Our first stop is the beauty salon. A frightening place filled with dozens of anxious females busily working on a quest to look younger.

I am perfectly happy with my image, thank you very much, but apparently Daddy Dearest is not—he has requested a "proper hairstyle" for me, whatever that might mean.

Yikes! I like my hair exactly the way it is: an abundance of wild curls that frame my face. My hair is me, it reflects my personality. I don't want anyone to mess with it.

A middle-aged gay man with firmly pursed lips and a pinched nose does not get the message—he goes to town on me, attempting to curl my hair into neat little girly curls.

I hate him. I hate the curls. Ugh! I emerge from his chair looking beyond hideous!

"You look adorable," Flora says, admiring her reflection in the mirror.

What does *she* know? Anyway, could be she's talking about herself, not me.

Next it's on to a fancy boutique, where Gino has personally chosen two dresses he wants me to have. One is shocking pink (yes, I kid you not!). It is frilled at the neck and hem. I can't even describe the other dress 'cause it's even worse.

"Mr. Santangelo has requested that you wear the pink one tonight," Flora says after I have tried the monstrosity on.

"No way," I protest, staring at myself in a full-length mirror. "It's hideous."

"Your father chose it personally," Flora says, adding a cloying "Surely you don't want to let him down?"

Yes I do. I do.

"And I guess I shouldn't tell you this," Flora adds, lowering her voice to a conspiratorial whisper. "Mr. Santangelo has a big surprise for you. I must say I'm quite envious."

A car, is it a car? I want to yell.

Now *that* would be true compensation for the hair and the dress.

"What is it?" I demand.

Flora giggles nervously. "I can't tell," she simpers. "It's a surprise."

Back at the hotel I sneak a shot of vodka from behind the bar, flirt with the room service waiter who delivers me a club sandwich, and play a game of lone pool on the full-size table. I'm pretty skillful at pool—if nothing else works out I can always be a pool hustler! Oh yeah, wouldn't everyone love that.

Gino's penthouse suite is like an amazing apartment—it even has an indoor-outdoor pool with fountains and a full music system. Talk about major luxury.

I explore the setup. Four bedrooms and that's not including Gino's. Why he needs four bedrooms, all with their own en-suite marble bathrooms, is beyond me. After Flora leaves I spend some time roaming around Gino's bedroom. There is a huge oversize bed, where he probably entertains an army of women. A giant TV that lowers from the ceiling. A Picasso painting on the wall. A closet full of clothes—including many of his favorite tailor-made suits, shirts galore, and dozens of silk ties in many colors. Daddy certainly knows how to look after himself. He has the best of everything.

I find myself wondering if he enjoys the fact that he has children—me and Dario. Or does he resent us?

Sad to say I honestly don't know.

~ ~ ~

Later, after I have brushed my hair back to some sort of normalcy, I put on the vile pink dress and wait until eventually Gino reappears. The good news is that he is with Marco!

Oh my God. Marco is all dressed up in a dinner jacket and black tie, and looks like a freaking movie star. I feel young and dumber than shit in my stupid dress. This is *not* the way I wanted Marco to see me. I am totally humiliated.

"Hey, kiddo," Gino says, hurrying to his room and calling over his shoulder. "Ten minutes an' we're outta here."

This leaves me and Marco alone in the vast living room with the mind-blowing view. I'm at a loss—what am I supposed to say?

I hover.

He ignores me.

I continue to hover.

He walks over to the bar, where he fixes himself a drink. Doesn't offer me anything. Doesn't say a word.

I wonder if he knows about Dario.

No. Why would he?

Should I tell him?

No. Why would I?

"This is my first Vegas trip," I venture, because the silence is just too awkward.

Marco gives me a long look. "Yeah?" he says, as if he couldn't care less.

I nod vigorously. "One day I'm going to be doing this," I add.

"Doing what?" he asks, still disinterested.

"Building hotels, making things happen."

"Don't you mean that's what your brother's gonna be doing?" Marco says. "Gino has big plans for Dario, he's gonna be the man."

I narrow my eyes. I am shocked. What the *hell* is he talking about? *I'm* the one who is going to inherit the family business. *I'm* the one with a million ideas for the future. Dario isn't interested in carrying on the family business. I know that for a fact because we've talked about it. Dario has absolutely no desire to follow in Gino's steps, he wants to write or paint. He's actually very artistic, so Marco is full of it.

"Dario has plans of his own," I mutter.

"Yeah?"

"Yes," I answer firmly.

Marco consults his watch. "We gotta go," he says, ignoring my comment about Dario's plans. "Mrs. Richmond doesn't enjoy being kept waiting."

"Who is she anyway?" I ask with a sulky scowl. "And why is Gino kissing her butt?"

"Gino doesn't kiss anyone's butt," Marco says with a dry laugh.

"Well, throwing a big event for her when it's *my* birthday, that's major sucking up."

Marco shrugs. "Gino does what he wants to do. Surely you've figured that out by now?"

I keep scowling, it feels good. I could get a master's in scowling.

"I'm never kissing up to anyone," I say with conviction. "They'll kiss my ass—and they'll love doing it."

Marco can't help grinning. White teeth flash. Sexy dark eyes. Deep olive skin like mine. I know we would have the most incredible-looking children.

"You're somethin', little Lucky," he drawls, staring me down. "You really are."

And I know for sure that I'm totally in love.

CHAPTER THIRTY-FOUR

The venue for Betty Richmond's event is massive, a vast ballroom filled with dozens of perfectly set-up tables with massive flower arrangements and an actual band playing on a stage. I gaze around in awe. Everyone appears to be rich and old, although the men seem to be a lot older than their female partners. What else is new?

As I trail behind Gino into the room, I notice Betty and Peter Richmond holding court. Gino immediately heads in their direction, and I start wondering where Marco is. He came downstairs with us and then vanished. I will him to reappear.

Biting my lip, I follow my father, feeling most uncomfortable in my stupid dress. Gino treats me as if I'm a kid always ready to do his bidding. It's time I straightened things out with him, let him know who I really am.

And who exactly is that? Oh yes, a smart sixteen-year-old who plans to rule the world, or at least the world of hotels and gambling in Vegas.

I want to be you, Daddy. I want the power. And one day I will have it.

Girls can do anything. This I know for sure.

Gino is now greeting Betty Richmond, kissing her on both cheeks, then shaking Senator Peter Richmond's hand.

And who's the tall, skinny jerk standing next to the Richmonds?

"Hey, kiddo," Gino says, turning to me. "Wancha t'meet Craven, Betty and Peter's son."

I give the tall one a quick scan. He's about twenty, and *so* not hot. He is horse-faced like his mom, with a ruddy complexion like his dad. He has ears that stick out, short hair, and a bad case of acne. I throw him a quick nod of acknowledgment. Too bad he's *not* hot, maybe we could've gotten into some trouble. But no, I can tell trouble is not on his radar.

Gino leads me over to a nearby table. "You'll be sitting here tonight," he informs me.

"With you?" I ask, although I already know the answer.

As usual Gino doesn't disappoint. "Sorry, kiddo," he says, not sounding sorry at all. "I gotta sit at the head table with the Richmonds. Craven's gonna be right next to you. I want you two kids t'get to know each other."

Huh. Is he joking? Craven Richmond is the last person I want to get to know. Before I can ask why he thinks I should get to know Craven, Marco reappears, passes Gino a small package, and sits himself down.

Things are suddenly looking up. Is Marco at my table? Yes! It seems he could be.

Gino shoves the package in his pocket, summons a waiter to bring over a bottle of champagne, and favors me with a benevolent smile. "You're a good kid at heart," he says. "An' here's the deal—you're gonna be okay."

I don't know what to say to that. It's not as if I have a terminal illness or anything—of course I'm going to be okay.

Recently I've decided I can handle anything: It's a powerful feeling and I'm sticking with it.

I slide a glance toward Marco. Surely it's not fair that one man can be so devastatingly handsome? Dark hair, dark eyes, and a look that women obviously find irresistible.

The champagne arrives, glasses are filled, and Gino clinks his with mine. "Happy birthday, kiddo," he says, digging into his pocket and pulling out the package Marco handed him earlier. He gives it to me. "For you, Princess," he adds.

I tear open the package. It contains an expensive-looking leather box. I open it and there, nestled against a velvet background, are two glittering diamond ear studs.

"Wow!" I gasp, throwing my arms around Gino and hugging him. "These are amazing!"

Chuckling, Gino pushes me gently away. "Thought you'd like 'em, kiddo."

I feel so damn happy. Here I am in Vegas on my birthday with my father, and he's just given me diamond earrings because he cares. He actually *does* love me. Things couldn't get any better.

"Those are some earrings," Marco remarks as I hold them up to my ears.

"I know," I gush. "So beautiful."

"Whyn't you go to the little girls' room an' put 'em on?" Gino suggests. "I wanna see what they look like on you."

I don't need asking twice. I jump up and practically run to the ladies' room, where I encounter Betty Richmond.

"Look what Daddy gave me," I blurt, flashing my earrings.

"That's nice," Betty says, although I can tell she doesn't mean it. For some unknown reason she obviously hates me.

Back at the table Gino is gone, so is Marco. The table is filling up with people I don't know. My burst of euphoria is on its way out, especially when Craven Richmond sits down next to me.

"How are you?" he asks.

A wave of bad breath envelops me. *Ugh!*

"Great," I mutter, and that's it for our conversational interaction.

~ ~ ~

A longer and more yawn-inducing event cannot possibly exist. Maybe I'm difficult to please, or maybe I don't have much patience, but the people at my table suck big-time. Nobody has anything to say, especially Craven, who I can't wait to escape from. He's the kind of guy Olympia and I would label jerk—creep—*boring*!

I wonder how Olympia's doing. I kind of miss her. She can be mean and selfish, but she's also the one responsible for encouraging me to be my own person.

"There's another party after this," Craven informs me. "Your father asked me to escort you to it."

Oh, he did, did he? What's wrong with you, Daddy? Why have you stuck me with this total idiot?

I agree to go because I find out it's Gino's party, which makes me sure that Marco will be there. And indeed he is, only *my* Marco is deep in conversation with some blonde bimbo in a too tight neon-orange dress.

I am outraged! What is he thinking? She's not his style at all. Too flashy and too trashy.

I throw Marco a steely glare before stalking around the room trying to locate Gino. When I do, I find he's too busy talking to the Richmonds to pay me any attention. So much for fatherly love.

Once more I hate him.

"I'm tired," I inform Craven, whom I can't seem to shake since he's obviously decided to follow me everywhere like an annoying shadow.

"Me, too," he agrees.

"Think I'll go to bed, then."

"I'll escort you to the elevator."

No escaping Craven and his bad breath. What did I do to deserve such a prince trailing me around?

We leave the party and mingle with the masses in the main lobby. I am dying to scoot into the casino to check it out—but Craven heads straight for the private elevator that'll whisk me up to Gino's penthouse.

We reach the elevator and stand there waiting for it to arrive.

"How about a game of tennis in the morning?" Craven asks, tapping the side of his long thin nose.

I feign a yawn and mumble, "Dunno what time I'll be up."

"I'll call you at ten," Craven says, not to be put off. Then before I can back away he leans over and kisses me chastely on the cheek, adding a cryptic "Don't worry, everything will turn out fine."

What?

I shake my head and quickly jump into the elevator.

Please God, make sure I never have to spend another evening with him again.

Craven Richmond brings dull to a whole new level.

CHAPTER THIRTY-FIVE

Home at last, or rather at Gino's luxurious Vegas penthouse, which is kind of creepy when there is nobody in it but me. My first move is to run into my bathroom, strip off my disgusting pink dress, crumple it in a ball, and kick it in a corner. Ha! I'm never wearing *that* again. Then I throw myself under a shower and wash the crimpy curls out of my hair.

The relief of becoming myself again works, and now I'm feeling as if I could manage some real fun. Gino thinks I'm safe somewhere with boring Craven. Flora is no longer around. So hey—I'm on my own. I can do what I like. And what I *don't* like is being cooped up. Freedom beckons, and believe me I'm on it!

Vegas calls.

Hello. I'm responding!

My next move is to fill up my bed with pillows so it

looks like I'm buried beneath them. Then I hide my diamond earrings somewhere safe, wriggle into my fave jeans, throw on a T-shirt, add smoky eyes and lip gloss to my face, pocket the key to the suite, and take off.

The private elevator whisks me to ground level and within seconds I'm mingling with the crowds.

The main lobby is packed with everyone from Hawaiian shirt–clad tourists to giggling groups of girls experiencing a bachelorette fun fest. It seems everyone is out to have a crazy time in Vegas. Tall, short, fat, and thin—they are all giggling and on the move.

I melt right in, getting lost in the crowds, although I soon decide it'll be safer for me to head for another hotel where I won't risk the chance of running into anyone who knows me.

I hurriedly make my way to the front of the hotel and follow the people spilling out onto the sidewalk, then I start walking.

This is so cool and I'm loving it! Little Lucky Saint no more. I am Lucky Santangelo, and one day I'm going to own this town. I'm going to build amazing hotels and casinos, just like Gino. Aunt Jen has told me the stories of how Gino came to Vegas right at the beginning when it first started. How he built his first hotel and casino, and got in on the ground floor along with notorious characters, including his partner Enzio Bonnatti, my godfather, a man we never seem to see anymore.

The next hotel I get to is even more jammed, with tons of people milling around in the enormous lobby decorated with lurid murals, huge statues, and splashing fountains.

I slink into the casino and hover near a bank of slot machines. Nobody stops me—guess I look as if I belong.

After throwing a few coins into one of the machines I hit a treble. Multiple coins pour out. I'm a winner! I don't win much, but I immediately realize that I'm on a roll and should follow up. Heading for the cashier, I change my coins into dollars, twenty dollars in all. Then I make it over to the roulette table and place my twenty on black.

Black comes up! I let it ride. Black comes up again!

So now I'm ahead eighty dollars in less than five minutes. Wow! So this is how gambling can become an addiction.

The croupier gives me a glassy stare. Is the old dude wondering how old I am? Is he about to question me?

Just in case, I scoop up my chips and move on. This is exciting stuff and I don't want to get busted for being underage.

After cashing in my chips, I wander from the casino into the huge gaudy lobby. Gino's hotel is much more tasteful—this one is way lower class, full of overweight people wearing flip-flops and shorts, with red faces and loud voices.

A couple of drunks clutching bottles of beer bump into me. "Whacha up to, pretty girl?" one snorts with a sloppy leer on his florid face.

I ignore them and keep walking.

"Stuck-up little bitch!" the second guy yells after me.

I turn around and give him the finger.

He shouts something obscene. I ignore him and carry on my merry way.

It's past midnight and I am free! I am in Vegas enjoying an adventure. *My* adventure, nobody else's. Talk about a feeling of lightness—I am positively floating!

Ah, if only Marco could see me now he'd realize I'm my own person, not some kid who has to do what Daddy tells her.

I decide to move on to the next hotel—nothing like exploring the city, getting the feel of it.

Once again—even though it's long past midnight—the sidewalk is crowded, everybody on their way somewhere. I guess in Vegas walking is the way to go if you want to stop by all the best hotels.

I marvel at the army of hotels lined up on the Strip, big flashy neon-lit palaces offering the chance to win a million bucks. The great American dream, and Gino has tapped into it big-time.

I am proud of my dad. I am proud to be his daughter. And I will be proud to carry on the Santangelo tradition, building even bigger and better hotels.

The yelp of an animal in pain catches my attention, and I notice some drunken vagrant squatting on the sidewalk beating on a cute little puppy with the back of a dirty sneaker.

Hell no! Not on my watch.

"Stop that!" I yell, determined to rescue the poor dog.

"Fuck off," the drunk mumbles, barely coherent. "Filthy bugger peed on me, gonna beat the crap outta the li'l shit."

"No way," I threaten, and before he can stop me I bend down and scoop up the puppy.

"Quit stealin' my property, thief!" the vagrant yells, grabbing my ankle with a bony hand, getting a firm grip.

The puppy scrambles in my arms, desperate to escape and go pee on someone else, while the vagrant tries his best to make me lose my balance, which I almost do until a man appears, gives the drunk a hefty kick, and pulls me away—puppy still in my possession.

Is it Marco to the rescue? For one insane moment I think it is. The man is tall and dark—but as he steers me down the street away from the drunk, I realize he's no Marco, although he is not bad-looking, in a shady kind of way.

"Thanks!" I gasp.

"Bit of advice," he offers. "Never mess with those assholes. They're covered in lice—not worth arguing with."

Hmm . . . like I need his advice.

The puppy barks. "Is this his dog?" I ask, as if he would know.

"Doubt it," the man says. "If I took a guess I'd say he probably stole it."

"Well," I venture, "what do you think I should do with it?"

"Put it down. If it's his it'll run back to him."

"I can't do that, he was beating it."

The man stares at me and I get a better look. He has brown eyes and a slightly crooked nose. Unshaven with a soul patch on his chin, he is obviously no boy, more like in his thirties. I reckon he's old, same as Marco, but not nearly as good-looking, although a whole lot better than Craven.

"What's a girl like you doing out on her own?" he asks.

"Rescuing dogs in peril," I reply tartly.

He laughs. "I suppose you wanna take the mutt to a shelter?"

"I wouldn't know where to go."

"Visiting?"

"Yes."

"By yourself?"

"Kind of."

"I can take you if you want."

Now I'm no dummy. A strange man on the Vegas Strip, not exactly a safe prospect. However, I consider myself a good enough judge of character, so what the hell, any funny stuff and I can handle myself.

"My car's parked round the corner," he says.

The puppy is wriggling big-time. "Okay," I agree.

He raises an eyebrow. "Trusting?"

I give it right back to him, show him that I'm not some dumb girl about to be taken advantage of. "My dad's a cop back in L.A.," I lie. "I think I can look after myself."

"Right on," the man says with a wolfish grin. "I'm Jeff, and you are?"

I decide not to give him my real name, so I come up with Maria, my mom's name.

"Maria." He repeats my name and scratches his chin. "Italian?"

"Sort of," I mutter, trying to control the rambunctious puppy, who is now determined to escape.

We walk down a side street to a parking lot where his car—a not-so-new Pontiac—is stashed. Vegas number-plates, I note.

"You from here?" I ask, boldly getting in the car.

"Born an' bred," he says. "Not many people can lay claim to that."

"What do you do?" I ask curiously.

"Blackjack dealer," he replies, lighting up a cigarette. "An' what do *you* do?"

I'm sixteen, asshole. I kind of go to school when they can keep me.

"Oh," I say, "a bit of this, a bit of that. My dad kinda wants me to train to be a cop."

"Sounds exciting," he says, inhaling deeply before blowing smoke in my general direction.

"Yeah, only I'm not sure," I say, waving the smoke out of my face.

He starts the engine. Miss Drew's warning words ring in my ears. "Never ever get into a car with a stranger. That's how young girls end up getting raped or even dead."

Thanks, Miss Drew, I'll bear that in mind.

"Do you know where to go?" I ask as he drives toward the Strip.

"There's an animal shelter downtown," he replies. "It's not too far. An' if you feel like it we can grab a beer an' play the slots at my favorite hotel."

"You have a favorite?"

"Yeah, it's a dump, only it's a helluva lot more welcoming than the big fancy places."

"Sounds good to me," I respond, feeling major cool and sophisticated. I have escaped Craven, and now I'm all set to have an interesting time with my new best friend. What could be better?

I'm free and I'm sixteen. And one day I *will* own this city.

CHAPTER THIRTY-SIX

Jeff turns out to be an okay guy. He's talkative and not bad-looking, although on closer inspection, he's definitely no Marco. After we deposit the puppy at the shelter, he drives us to a downtown honky-tonk joint, jammed with grungy offbeat characters and girls who could be hookers in their tight leopard-print shorter-than-short skirts, fishnet tights, and sky-high heels. A cocktail waitress wearing very little gives Jeff a warm greeting, which I suppose is a good sign. There're several pool tables and a bank of slot machines, both of which we play. I cream him at pool, which doesn't thrill him. Neither of us hit any jackpots. Too bad. As I guzzle down my third glass of cheap wine followed by a beer, I'm glad I trusted him—he seems like fun, and I am in dire need of some fun.

After a while he asks if I'm hungry—which I am—and we move on to a fast-food place where he scores me a big fat juicy burger and french fries. I wolf everything down as if I haven't eaten in a month. Not very ladylike, but then I'm not a very ladylike sort of girl.

"What's it like being a dealer?" I ask, chewing on my burger as if it's my last meal.

He shrugs. "Not bad when the tipping goes my way."

"And does it?"

"What?"

"Go your way."

A sly grin and a wink. "The women customers can be very generous, if you get my drift."

"Do you, like, manipulate the cards?" I ask curiously.

He throws me a quizzical look. "What kind of question is *that*?"

"Just asking," I say, drowning a french fry in ketchup and stuffing it in my mouth.

"You're full of surprises."

"I am?"

"If I didn't know better, I'd think you were a spy for one of the casino managers, or maybe a pool hustler."

I stifle a giggle. If he only knew my real identity, he'd crap himself!

"You got beautiful eyes," he says.

Ah, the come-on is about to begin, and not a moment too soon. It's been way too long since "almost" with Jon, and I am hot to get some good healthy necking in.

He reaches forward and touches my hair.

I feel a tingle of anticipation.

"We should get outta here," he smirks, confident he's

onto a sure thing. "My apartment's nearby. Wanna see my collection of Indian relics?"

Indian relics? Is he kidding me?

"Can't," I say, trying to sound genuinely regretful, 'cause getting in his car is one thing, but there's no way I'm about to get trapped in his apartment. "Gotta get back to my hotel. It's late, and I have to be up early. My dad's driving in to meet me from L.A. He gets livid if I keep him waiting."

This doesn't sit too well with Jeff. Obviously he was expecting a burger and fries would buy him a long lustful night of sex.

Sorry again, dude. But finding myself a prisoner in your apartment is not for me. No way.

"Too bad," he says at last.

"Yeah," I agree, putting on a sorry face.

"Well, anyway," he adds, "at least I can drive you to your hotel."

Hmm . . . decision time . . . Do I get in the car again with him or not?

I decide yes. Nothing wrong with a little making out in a car.

And that is exactly what happens. He drives me to Gino's hotel, parks in the back lot, and then we start to go at it. Kissing, groping, fumbling, touching.

He is so *not* a skillful kisser. His lips are plummy and soft like a girl's, and his mouth tastes of stale beer. As for his hands, they are big and rough and all over me.

I realize I have made a big mistake. "Almost" with this dude is not for me.

"Gotta go," I gasp, reaching for the door handle.

"Huh?" he mumbles.

I jump out of the car. He jumps out after me.

"You can't go," he says, circling around me.

"I think I can," I respond, edging away from him.

He pins me up against a brick wall and attempts to kiss me again.

I shove him away. "I *said* I've gotta go," I repeat.

"An' leave me like this?" he groans, pressing himself hard against me. "Y'know, there's a name for girls like you."

Before I realize it, he's unzipping his fly, and his hands start groping under my T-shirt.

Oh wow! I attempt to get away. It is not possible because he still has me pinned against the wall. I'm not scared, but I *am* starting to get mad, especially when he starts ripping at the fastening of my jeans, almost pulling them down.

Time for the famous Santangelo knee to the groin, a move I excel at. I give it to him hard and fast.

He is surprised, then furious, letting out a sharp cry of pain. But by that time I am on the run, pulling up my jeans and leaving him way in the distance.

I dodge between legions of parked cars and make a beeline for the hotel.

Whew! Close call, but I handled it in true Santangelo fashion.

When I reach the front of the hotel I slow down—there's no way he's following me. It's four A.M. and I am safe and sound. Time to sneak back upstairs to Gino's penthouse and fall into bed. Sleep beckons; it's been a long night.

"Lucky?"

Someone is calling my name, and it can't be my attacker because he doesn't even know my real name.

"Lucky?" The voice gets nearer.

I glance over my shoulder, and *oh my God*, it's Marco. The real Marco, not some useless carbon copy.

"Oh!" I gasp. "It's you."

He's staring at me like I'm some kind of alien. "What are you doin' out at this time?"

"Uh . . ." A quick think. "Um . . . couldn't sleep, so I took a walk."

"A walk. Where?"

"Just around."

I can tell he is checking me out, and I know I must look like a total wreck.

"Does Gino know you're out?" he questions, a stern glint in his eyes.

"Gino was asleep," I answer vaguely. "Didn't want to disturb him."

Marco shakes his head. *Oh my God, he is so damn handsome.* "Baby," he says, "if Gino knew you were out, you'd disturb him all right."

The way he says "baby" makes me shiver. I love him, I love him, I LOVE HIM!

"I'm hungry," I say, taking the most of this opportunity to be alone with him. "Is there anywhere I can get a sandwich?"

"I'll have one sent up to you," he says.

"But I don't feel like going up yet," I respond.

Marco looks perplexed. Why is *he* up at four A.M.? I start to wonder where *he's* been. Probably with that skank from the party. She doesn't deserve him. *I* do.

"You don't, huh?"

"Nope."

"Okay, Lucky," he decides. "I'll take you to the coffee shop."

Brilliant!

We make our way there, and I am psyched.

"Uh . . . I don't think you should tell Gino I was out," I venture as we settle into a booth facing each other.

Marco throws me a steely look. "You don't, huh?"

I nod my head vigorously. "Y'know how Gino gets."

"Yeah, I do know."

I lean toward him. "So . . . this can be our secret, right?"

Marco scratches his chin with his index finger. "You seem kind of messed up, Lucky. Were you drinkin'?" he asks, giving me a penetrating stare.

"Me?" I say, all innocent.

"Yeah, you."

"No way," I say, conveniently forgetting about the three or four beers plus the wine I'd consumed earlier.

"You're sure?"

"Of course I'm sure."

Marco seems to be thinking, then he gets up and informs me he'll be right back.

I am concerned. Surely he hasn't gone to call Gino? Oh God, Gino will *not* be happy.

But no, Marco returns within minutes, orders a glass of water, and watches me while I consume a chicken sandwich. I am not really hungry, but spending alone-time with Marco is worth stuffing myself.

"Y'know, Lucky," Marco says thoughtfully. "This is a dangerous town. A pretty young girl like you has to be careful."

He called me pretty! Marco called me pretty!

"I don't need a lecture," I mumble, chewing on my sandwich. "And I can assure you, I *do* know how to look after myself."

"Gino happens to be a very important man in this city," Marco continues. "What you get up to reflects directly on him."

I shrug. "Then it's good I'm not getting up to anything, right?" I counter.

He nods unsurely. "Right."

I beam at him. "This is terrific," I say boldly. "We should do this more often."

CHAPTER THIRTY-SEVEN

Marco escorts me upstairs to the door of Gino's pent-house suite. I am euphoric—being with Marco, just the two of us, has made the whole Vegas trip worthwhile. He is *it* for me. The perfect man. I am in a bit of a trance as I reach for the key tucked into the back pocket of my jeans. "Shhh . . ." I whisper. "Mustn't wake Big Daddy."

Marco is silent.

"I'd ask you in," I continue, "but I guess *he* wouldn't like it." Then, feeling even bolder, I go for the gold. "Of course, you *could* ask me back to *your* room—"

"Good night, Lucky," Marco says, frowning. "Go sleep it off, you'll feel better in the morning."

"What?" I say, grabbing him. "No good-night kiss?" And before he can dodge me, I press my mouth firmly against his.

Unfortunately he does not seem to appreciate this move 'cause he backs off real quick and heads for the elevator.

Just in time, for once again my name is called, and this time it's my father, Gino, an angry man in a white terry-cloth bathrobe, a ferocious expression on his face.

"Where you bin, kid?" Gino demands in a harsh voice. "Out gettin' laid?"

I am totally startled. How dare he talk to me as if I'm some kind of tramp?

"Daddy . . ." I stutter, as Marco vanishes into the elevator.

Gino's black eyes rake me over from head to toe, and I know he misses nothing. I pull down my T-shirt and shy away from his scrutiny.

"You think I was born yesterday, kid," he rasps. "You think I don't know what goes on out there."

"Out where?" I say lamely.

"Y'know what I mean."

"I'm sorry," I mutter.

"Don't go givin' me that sorry shit again," he says, glaring at me. "I've had it with that crap. It don't work no more. Who exactly d'you think you're foolin'?"

"I just went for a walk, that's all," I say with a defensive shrug. "There's no law against doing that."

"A walk, my ass," Gino says harshly. "Is that why your hair an' clothes are such a mess? An' how about the bruises all up your arms. A walk, huh?"

"A man attacked me," I blurt. "I was wandering around the parking lot and he jumped me."

"No shit," Gino says, shaking his head.

"Yes, really," I say, wide-eyed.

"Guess it was just like that boy in Switzerland, huh? The boy who accordin' t'you just happened to turn up in your room, strip off, an' climb in bed with you—the both of you bare-assed. While across the room your so-called friend was doin' the same thing." An ominous pause, then: "I've bin meanin' t'ask, how come neither of you screamed for help? Answer me that."

Should I answer Gino, or simply let him rave on? I stare moodily at the floor. It's black and white marble, very cold and pristine.

All I can think about is Marco, and the way he betrayed me. What a dick.

"An' let's not forget France," Gino continues, still glaring at me. "You and your whore friend shacked up in the villa with a goddamn pimp. How many guys didja have there? How many, kid? Or did you an' your friend settle for sharin' the services of the pimp?"

Tears fill my eyes. *It's my sixteenth birthday, Daddy, cut me a break.*

"It wasn't like that," I mutter.

"Enough with the crap excuses," Gino steams, his eyes an angry deadly black. "No daughter of mine is gonna be runnin' round town actin' like a *putana*. I finally figured out what I'm gonna do with you, an' you should get down on your knees an' thank me."

"What?" I whisper fearfully.

"You got hot pants, you wanna fuck around, so be it. Only you're not doin' it on my fuckin' watch. You're Gino

Santangelo's daughter, and you'd better learn to respect that."

"I don't fuck around," I mumble, humiliated and upset. "Honestly, Daddy, I don't."

"I'm marryin' you off, kid. I've found you the right husband an' you're gettin' married, so any screwin' around you do will be in your marriage bed an' nowhere else."

"W . . . what?" I stammer, not quite sure I've heard him correctly.

"You heard me, an' you'd better understand what I'm sayin', 'cause you got no choice."

I'm trembling. This is total disaster time.

"I don't want to get married," I hear myself saying.

"Too bad," he says sternly.

I feel color creeping into my face. Why is he like this? Why doesn't he love me?

"You're nothing but a big stupid bully," I spit, full of venom. "You don't understand me, and you never will. It's 'cause of you Mommy got murdered. I *hate* you."

Instantly Gino lashes out and whacks me across the face. I spin across the hallway, such is his strength. We are both shocked.

Within seconds Gino comes after me and cradles me in his arms. "I'm sorry, kiddo," he croons. "I didn't mean to do that, only you gotta realize you're so goddamn stubborn, exactly like me. I only want what's best for you. You're my little princess, an' if *I* don't protect you, who will?"

Deep in the warmth of his arms I start to cry. He called

me his little princess. He cares, he really cares. I'm Daddy's little girl. I'm five years old and we're playing games and having fun. Mommy is there, smiling at us, beautiful Mommy Maria. Security envelops us, and not in a bad way.

I breathe in Gino's smell. Daddy's smell, a mixture of aftershave and warmth. I'm in his arms and I love him. I will do anything he wants me to do, because he loves me as much as I love him.

"Okay, Daddy," I whisper. "I'll listen to you. I'll do it. I'll do anything to make it right between us."

"That's my girl," he says soothingly, stroking the hair off my face. "It'll be for the best, you'll see. I'm protecting you, sweetheart, protecting you from yourself."

Suddenly I realize the blazing truth—he is marrying me off to Marco. Of course he is. And for one shining moment all is right in the world.

"Who?" I ask softly. "Who am I marrying?"

"Craven Richmond," Gino announces proudly. "It's all arranged."

CHAPTER THIRTY-EIGHT

My stomach drops as if the world is ending. Did Gino just say Craven Richmond? No. That's impossible. I misheard him. Surely he uttered Marco's name?

I pull away from my father and stare at him in disbelief.

"I don't even *know* Craven Richmond," I mutter, still feeling the sting of Gino's slap across my face.

"Doesn't matter, you'll get to know him," Gino says, as if it's no big deal. "You gotta get it into your head, he's a catch, kiddo. His family is political royalty."

I am stunned. Political royalty, what does *that* mean?

"Go to bed, an' we'll talk in the mornin'," Gino says, like he hasn't just dropped this horrendous bombshell on me.

"But Daddy—" I begin.

Too late. He's walking away, leaving me crushed.

I make it to my room and throw myself on the circular

bed. Everything is one big surreal blur. I'm sixteen and about to be married off to some jerk I don't even know. What am I to do? Should I run? Make a daring escape?

And go where?

I start to collect my thoughts. There's no way Gino can force me to go through with this. We're not in some country where arranged marriage is the norm. We're in America—land of the free. I can do whatever I want.

Then I start considering the alternatives.

School.

No thank you.

Homeschooling.

Even worse.

Then if not school—what?

Daddy Dearest has made it clear he doesn't want me working alongside him. According to him I'm just a girl. Only boys get that privilege.

One of these days I will make him change his mind. I know I can do it.

So what if I do get married to Craven? Play the good little wife until I'm older and ready to strike. At least it will give me the independence I crave. And who says I have to stay married?

I curl up into a ball and attempt to sleep, but it's almost impossible 'cause my mind is on speed dial.

Marriage or school?

Not much of a choice.

~ ~ ~

By the time I awake it is almost noon and I'm not in great shape. I am most likely experiencing my first real hangover.

Memories of the previous evening explode in my brain. The Richmond event. Diamond earrings from Daddy. Boring Craven Richmond. My walk on the wild side. Horny Jeff. Handsome Marco. Big Daddy Gino.

Marriage!!!

Mrs. Craven Richmond. Lucky Richmond. Neither of them sound right.

Who are the Richmonds anyway? He's some kind of big-deal senator, and apparently she's a do-gooder, heavy on the charity circuit if last night is anything to go by.

How does Gino even *know* them? I need to find out.

After showering and throwing on my jeans, I go looking for Gino. A maid is in his bedroom making up his bed.

"Where's my father?" I demand.

She stares at me unsurely. "No Engleesh," she finally says.

Has he left Vegas, flown away and dumped me?

No, Gino wouldn't do that. I'm to be married, there are arrangements to be made.

I return to my room. The message light on the phone is blinking. Tentatively I pick up. The first message is from boring Craven mumbling about a tennis game. Too late for that, it's almost noon.

The second message is from Marco, the Betrayer. "Lucky," he says, sounding strained. "Gino had a couple of meetings he had to go to. Call me when you're up."

Hmm . . . did the kiss I gave him work? Is he ready to seal the deal and rescue me from Craven?

I have a feeling not. Anyway, I hate him now. He must've known what Gino had planned, so why didn't he warn me?

I pick up the phone and call him. "Yes, Marco?" I say, as icy as I can make it.

"How're you feelin'?" he asks.

What does *he* care?

"Just great," I say sarcastically. "Thanks for blowing my cover, so loyal of you."

"Hey, Lucky, I did what was best for you."

"Yeah," I snap. "Right."

"Gino has arranged for you to meet with Mrs. Richmond today."

"What for?"

"To discuss everything."

"You mean to discuss my so-called upcoming arranged marriage?"

"It's not such a bad thing, Lucky. Craven's a nice guy."

"How do you know?"

"Uh, I can tell."

I suddenly lose it. Marco the Betrayer is no longer my would-be lover. He's a freaking jerk and I hate him.

"Y'know, Marco," I hiss, narrowing my eyes, "one of these days you're going to realize what you're missing, and believe me, you'll be *real* sorry, only by that time it'll be too late, so *there!*"

I slam down the phone. A fleeting moment of triumph before the phone rings. I snatch it up.

"Four o'clock in the Patio Room," Marco says flatly. "Flora will pick you up. Try not to keep Mrs. Richmond waiting."

Then he is gone. *My* Marco no more.

Damn him.

Damn the whole freaking lot of them.

~ ~ ~

Mrs. Richmond is clad in Chanel from head to toe—even her two-tone shoes bear the designer label.

She sits at a table in the Patio Room, sipping tea and looking as if she's experiencing a bad smell. Obviously this match between me and Craven does not thrill her.

I can't help wondering what power Gino has over the Richmonds to make this happen. Something is going down, and I have no clue what it could be.

"Lucky, dear," Betty Richmond says, a fake smile plastered on her frozen face. "Do sit. Might I order you some tea?"

I slouch into a chair. I am wearing jeans, combat boots, and a denim shirt. Earlier Flora arrived at Gino's penthouse followed by a man pushing a rack of dresses. I'd refused to wear any of them.

"I'll have a Coke," I mutter.

"So bad for you, all that caffeine," Betty scolds.

Like I care what the old bag thinks.

"So," Betty says, adjusting a discreet pearl earring. "We have much to organize."

For a moment I realize the insanity that's going on here. I hardly *know* Craven Richmond, and he's certainly not proposed to me. Yet here I am, sitting with his mother, about to discuss our wedding. It's crazy and kind of funny all at the same time. I experience an insane desire to laugh out loud. But I don't. I remain straight-faced.

"I have hired a wedding planner who is on her way here from Washington," Betty announces with a flourish. "She's an extremely capable woman who will make sure every-thing runs as smoothly as possible." A long pause, followed by—"However, as you know, time is of the essence."

What? I don't get it. Why is time of the essence? It's not as if I'm pregnant or anything. The truth is I'm still a virgin, so lucky Craven. Yippee for the wedding night!

"Tonight you and Craven are to enjoy a quiet dinner together," Betty Richmond continues. "My son will have a selection of rings for you to choose from. I picked them out myself—I'm sure you'll find something that pleases you."

Wow! Is this really happening? Where's Olympia when I need her?

Help, help, *help*! It would be nice to have a friend to lean on.

"Apart from the wedding planner, I have arranged for my personal stylist to assist you in your choice of dress for the happy day. He will also be flying in. You will honeymoon in the Bahamas, everything is arranged." She pauses again and licks her thin lips. "Now, dear, do you have any questions?"

Yes. Why is this happening?

"Uh . . . no," I stutter.

"I realize this is all taking place extremely fast," Betty says, dead eyes flickering. "However, this is the way Gino wants it, and we all know that when Gino wants something it is bound to happen."

Yes, we all know that.

"Okay, then," I mumble, sipping my Coke. "I guess everything is set."

Betty nods her perfectly coiffed head. "It certainly is, dear. Your transformation will begin tomorrow with Raoul, my stylist. Try to wear something suitable for your dinner with Craven tonight, I'm sure he will appreciate it."

Transformation? What the hell!

They can force me into a marriage, but they cannot take away who I am. And that's for sure.

CHAPTER THIRTY-NINE

I don't dress for dinner. Why should I? Isn't it enough that I'm agreeing to this farce of a marriage? Gino wants me to marry Craven Richmond, and he wants me to do it fast. According to Betty Richmond, within the next ten days!

A shotgun wedding with no shotgun involved. *Hmm* . . .

Why is everyone on board with this? Why are the Richmonds sacrificing their only son? Not that Craven is much of a sacrifice. He seems like a dolt, a nerd, a nonentity. Perhaps they realize he needs a girl like me to push him to be someone other than Peter Richmond's boy.

Suddenly I am getting into this whole scenario. I will be Sadie Sadie Married Lady—and then I can do whatever I like. However, I am determined to find out how Gino has orchestrated this whole thing.

I pick up the phone and call Aunt Jen in New York. "Did you know about this?" I ask, curious to find out what she has to say.

She waffles on, tells me that Gino is only doing this to protect me from myself, and that I should be thankful he's so concerned about me.

I love Aunt Jen, but she's not the smartest cookie in the jar.

"Do you *know* the Richmonds?" I ask.

"We had dinner with the senator and Gino," Aunt Jen says, sounding vague. "Let me see, it was when Gino was dating that famous movie star—what was her name again?"

"Marabelle Blue?"

"Yes, lovely woman."

I am curious. "Marabelle was friendly with the senator, too?" I ask.

Aunt Jen suddenly goes all evasive, which immediately gives me cause to be suspicious.

"I'm not sure," she says, then quickly changes the subject. "Costa and I will be flying in for your wedding. We're very excited for you." She lowers her voice. "It really *is* for the best, Lucky. You're very mature for your years. It's time for you to settle down. Gino knows what's right for you.'

And if they think that settling down is what I'm going to do, then they'd better all think again. Because this girl has plans. Major plans.

~ ~ ~

Craven is waiting for me at the Polynesian restaurant in the hotel. He leaps up when he spots me approaching, almost knocking a tall vase of flowers off the table. He'd wanted to meet me at the bottom of the elevator, but I'd demurred, saying I would see him at the restaurant.

What a strange situation I am caught up in. Yet I'm feeling kind of in control and powerful—I'm not sure why.

"Good evening, Lucky," Craven says in a choked-up voice.

"Hey," I reply. I haven't chosen to wear one of those disgusting dresses hanging in my room, but I have put on a short skirt and a black sweater. My hair is wild as usual, and my diamond earrings flash nicely.

"You look b . . . beautiful," Craven stammers.

"Thanks," I say, sitting opposite him instead of sliding onto the banquette next to him.

"I'm s . . . s . . . sorry we couldn't play tennis this morning."

I shrug as if it doesn't matter. "I'm not a very good tennis player, anyway. You'd probably have beaten me."

"Mother is a ch . . . ch . . . champion," he boasts. "She always wins."

"I bet," I say, stifling a random yawn.

"Mother is an excellent sportswoman. Golf, swimming, skiing."

"Wow!"

"Do you play golf?"

"Isn't that a game for old people?"

"Mother finds it invigorating."

"Well, I'd sooner catch a movie."

Polite conversation is now taking place between two people who don't even know each other, but will shortly be a married couple. And all Craven can do is praise his dear old mom. Bizarro!

I wonder if he's going to propose. How awkward will *that* be.

Fortunately he doesn't. Instead, later in the evening he produces a tray of rings and suggests I choose two. "An engagement r . . . r . . . ring and a w . . . w . . . wedding band," he stammers, red in the face.

The truth is I feel sorry for him. He's not any kind of threat, and he sure as hell isn't sexy. He seems introverted and devastatingly shy. And then there's the stammer.

I inspect the rings. Not my style, but I choose a nice-size diamond and a thin gold wedding band.

Nervously he leans across the table and slips the engagement ring on my finger.

"For you," he says.

"Thanks," I reply, wondering if there's any chance of making a run for it later and hitting the town.

The rest of the dinner is uneventful. Craven continues to talk about his mother, a lot—it's as if in his mind she's some kind of supergoddess who can do no wrong. I note he doesn't have much to say about Peter, his father. If I was to hazard a guess, I'd say that Peter finds him to be a big disappointment.

"Are you interested in following your dad into politics?"

I inquire, thinking what it might be like to be a political wife. I could conquer Washington instead of Vegas. What a trip *that* would be.

Craven shakes his head. I decide that he needs to grow his hair—the way he has it cut now does not flatter him.

"Not at all," he says firmly. "Never."

"What do you do now?" I ask curiously. And I have a hundred more questions such as—*Where will we live? Who are your friends? What are your hobbies? Are you into travel? Have you ever had sex?*

"I work with Mother on her charity events," Craven says with a proud smirk. "She r . . . r . . . raises millions for excellent causes."

Oh crap! That sounds like a shitload of laughs.

"Surely you want more?" I venture.

"More than what?" he says with a slight frown.

"More than just being your mom's errand boy."

I've offended him. He throws me a hurt look and clams up.

"I know what *I* want," I announce. "I plan on following in *my* father's footsteps. Gino builds amazing hotels, and one day I'm doing the same."

"You'll need plenty of money for that."

"I can raise it," I say confidently. "I'll put together a bunch of investors who will definitely share my vision. It's not that difficult."

"Mother says that women shouldn't work unless it's for a good cause."

I raise a caustic eyebrow. Is he kidding me? "That's a very antiquated point of view," I say sharply. "Kinda dumb actually."

"It's the way the world is," Craven replies, a smug look on his face.

No stutter when he's sure of what he's saying. Interesting.

"Can I ask you something?" I venture.

"Go right ahead," he says, his expression still smug.

"Why exactly are you doing this?"

My question throws him.

"Doing w . . . w . . . what?" he stammers.

"Marrying me, of course."

He shifts uncomfortably. "You're very pretty," he says at last.

"So is our waitress," I point out.

"Mother th . . . thinks we will be a good match. She *wants* me to be married."

"How convenient."

"What?"

"Gino's desperate to marry me off 'cause he considers me out of his control. I'm interested to find out what kind of deal he made with your parents to throw *you* into the mix?"

Craven manages to look pained. "There is no deal. Mother s . . . s . . . says we will grow to love each other. Her only wish is to see me happy."

"Hmm . . ." I murmur.

"I do like you, Lucky," he adds with a sincere nod. "You're very different from other girls."

"Have you had a lot of girlfriends?" I ask curiously, although I think I already know the answer.

He looks down. "Not really," he mutters.

Oh, big surprise. I'm dying to ask him if he's ever had sex, but I figure now is not the appropriate time.

We finish our dinner with a chocolate soufflé, quite delicious actually. Then Craven escorts me to the elevator and I receive another chaste kiss on the cheek.

I'm busy thinking about what I might get up to later. Maybe roam the streets and soak in the Vegas sights and sounds. It's a plan.

However, once I get upstairs I note a security guard stationed outside the penthouse.

Dammit! Gino's got my number. No escape for me tonight.

CHAPTER FORTY

"How'd your dinner go?" Gino asks. We are sitting at the breakfast table on the terrace of his penthouse, the first time I've seen him since he announced my upcoming nuptials.

"Okay," I reply, flashing my diamond engagement ring in his face. "Got this."

"He's a generous kid," Gino remarks.

"Betty Richmond chose it."

"She has good taste."

"You think?"

"Craven is a nice boy," Gino says, picking up his coffee cup.

Craven is a total mommy's boy, I'm dying to shout, but I don't. I've decided to play Gino's game, because I have a hunch that going along with it is my first step on the road to freedom. Right now I'm a teenager with no rights. Soon I will be a married woman who can do whatever she wants.

"How well do you know him?" I ask.

"Well enough," Gino replies.

"Oh," I say, sure that Gino doesn't know him at all.

"Got a surprise for you, kiddo," Gino says.

Oh, like the arranged marriage isn't enough of a surprise?

"What?" I ask, adding a hopeful "Is it a car, 'cause I really need a car."

Gino laughs. "Is that what you want?"

I nod.

"So I'll buy you a car as a wedding present," he announces. "Deal?"

"Can I choose it?" I ask, jumping at the opportunity to get something I really want.

"Yeah, sure," Gino says amiably.

Seems to me that Gino is so pleased that I'm going along with this wedding deal that he's prepared to give me anything I ask for. Obviously it's time to take advantage.

"I'd like a Ferrari," I say, going for it big-time. "A red one."

"Nix on a Ferrari, kiddo," Gino says with a chuckle. "More like a family car, 'cause before you know it you'll be raisin' a family."

Oh, how well he doesn't know me!

A quick switch of subjects. "What's the surprise?"

"I've arranged for Dario to fly in."

Good news at last! Dario, baby brother, someone I can bond with.

"When?" I ask.

"He'll be here tomorrow."

I am excited. I miss my brother so much, and I need to share with him why I've decided to go through with this sham. He'll understand. He always does.

"When are we going back to L.A.?" I inquire, not so anxious to stay in Vegas anymore.

"We're not," Gino states with a note of puzzlement in his voice. "Didn't anyone tell you? The weddin's takin' place here in Vegas."

No, Daddy, nobody told me. Why would they? It's only my wedding.

"I need to get back to L.A. All my stuff's there," I insist.

"Call Miss Drew. She'll bring anythin' you want. She'll be here in a coupla days."

This sucks. What I *want* are my clothes and my personal items. The teddy bear Mommy gave me when I was three. My journals, books, photos, clothes. My whole life is in L.A. I don't care for the thought of Miss Drew rooting through my personal possessions.

Why is this happening to me? Why am I being isolated in Vegas unable to do anything except go along with a planned wedding? Is now the time to rebel, inform Gino I'm not doing it?

No, my inner voice warns me. *The alternative is another school, more authority. This way you'll be free.*

Well, I think, *kind of.* I'll be married to Craven, but I've already figured out that he's no threat. I can control him once I get him out of Betty Richmond's clutches.

"I don't see why I can't fly back to L.A. for a day," I complain with one of my famous scowls. "It's not as if it's a big deal. It's only an hour on a plane."

"Settle down," Gino says, trying to calm me.

"Why should I?" I retort.

Before Gino can reply, Marco appears.

Ah, my betrayer, handsome as ever, but my love for him has turned sour.

"Mornin', Lucky," he says, handing Gino a large thick envelope.

I ignore him and concentrate on buttering a slice of toast.

One of these days, Marco, you will be sorry you treated me like a dumb little kid. Ah yes, eventually I will have revenge.

Gino weighs the sturdy envelope in his hands. He grins at Marco. "Business must be boomin'," he says.

"It was a good night," Marco responds. "The Asians were out in force."

"As always," Gino agrees.

"Yeah, they love losin' their money," Marco says, rubbing his hands together.

"Fortunate for us," Gino says with a sly grin.

I wonder what's in the envelope.

Cash, of course.

I wonder how much cash.

A lot.

"Join us," Gino says to Marco. "Sit down, grab yourself a coffee."

Marco shoots me a look. I refuse to meet his eyes. "Got a meeting," he says.

Am I making him uncomfortable? Good. I sincerely hope so.

"Well, kiddo." Gino turns to me as Marco leaves. "Your future mother-in-law has got the weddin' planner flyin' in today. She's arranged for the two of you to spend the day with her tomorrow."

"Why?" I look at him blankly.

"To make decisions," Gino replies a tad impatiently.

"What decisions?" I ask, purposely being obtuse.

"How would I know?" he snaps. "Food, flowers, crap like that."

Ah, my father is so damn eloquent.

"I'm not interested in the details," I say grandly. "I'm sure Mrs. Richmond can handle everything. She doesn't need my help."

"Suit yourself," Gino says with an I'm-not-getting-involved shrug.

Oh I will, Daddy, I will.

~ ~ ~

Later Gino goes to his safe to stash the envelope of cash Marco handed him.

I have discovered that his safe is located behind the Picasso in his bedroom. I discovered this by spying on him when he left the breakfast table. I'd make an excellent spy. Quiet and stealthy.

"You seein' Craven today?" he asks, before he leaves the penthouse.

Craven has already called and invited me to lunch—I declined, pleading a headache.

"Probably," I reply, although I have no intention of doing so.

"Yeah," Gino says with an affirming nod. "I knew you two kids would get along. I gotta hunch 'bout these things. You'll make a great couple."

Bull . . . *shit*, Daddy. I have to find out what's in it for you other than getting me off your hands.

As soon as he leaves I check for any hovering housekeepers. All clear. I take a deep breath and make it into Gino's bedroom.

The Picasso stares at me, a wild configuration of bright colors and odd shapes.

I stare back.

Hello, painting. What deep, dark secrets are you guarding?

I slide the painting out of the way and confront a large safe. It will not be pleasant if I'm caught doing this, but I've put the security lock on the main door to the penthouse, so nobody can get in without pressing the buzzer for attention.

Hmm . . . how am I supposed to open the formidable-looking safe? I am adept at many things—however, safecracking is not one of them.

I remember the safe Gino has in his study at the Bel Air

house. I remember him opening it once when I was in the room. I remember noting the numbers he used, even though I was only eleven at the time: 7 7 7 8 8 8. So simple.

Of course he must've changed the code since then. But what the hell, I decide to give it a try anyway. And bingo! To my total surprise the large safe clicks open.

I am both startled and exhilarated.

C'mon, Gino! This is a bonus. What will I discover, that is the question.

CHAPTER FORTY-ONE

Money. Cash. Stacks of it. Hundreds and thousands of dollars. A box full of delicate jewelery—maybe it was Mommy's? Why is he holding on to it? Why isn't he giving it to me?

There are two handguns and several boxes of ammunition. A clutch of expensive watches. A dozen gold coins.

Another box—this time full of photos, photos that make me want to cry. Gino and Maria on their wedding day. Such a beautiful couple, Maria—my mom—so young, only a few years older than me. And Gino, handsome and charismatic. My parents. Memories of my mother murdered in the family swimming pool come rushing back. I push them away and continue to search the safe.

Next I find a separate eight-by-ten manila envelope which reveals nude photos of Marabelle Blue, and not the artistic kind one sees in men's magazines.

I stare at them, feeling like a total voyeur. I wish I hadn't investigated this particular envelope.

Finally I discover another envelope tucked right at the back of the safe, marked "The Richmond File."

My pulse races. Am I about to hit pay dirt? Is this what I've been looking for?

I have a strong hunch it is.

My hand shakes as I open the envelope. I am filled with guilt as I snoop through Gino's private things. But I'm entitled, aren't I? Surely I should know why I'm being delivered to the Richmond family on a silver platter.

Yes. I have rights.

I open the envelope, and for some strange reason I am not surprised by what I see.

Gino's ammunition.

Gino's hold over the Richmonds.

A series of graphic bedroom photos of the senator and the movie star.

Oh my God! And I *do* mean graphic.

I take a gulp of air and quickly stuff the photos back in the envelope. So this is what Gino has. Blackmail material against Peter Richmond.

I immediately wonder if Betty has seen the photos? She must have, because why else would she have so readily agreed to the marriage between me and her precious son?

Oh yes, I get it. Gino courts power, legitimate power, so he sets up his movie-star girlfriend with the senator and nabs the pics. That way, when he wants a favor, Peter will oblige big-time—otherwise Gino will release the photos to the press, and ruin Peter's chance of ever running for president. I know the way my father thinks. After all, I'm a Santangelo, too.

So . . . I'm out of control in Gino's eyes, he doesn't have a clue what to do with me. And then it all clicks. Marry me off to the senator's boring son and we'll all be one big dysfunctional happy family!

Everyone wins.

Except me.

Although I have already decided that I can work this to my advantage. I'm not a kid anymore, and once I'm married nobody will regard me as one.

Hastily I put everything back the way I found it, close the safe, and adjust the Picasso to its rightful place.

To say I am filled with a feeling of triumph would be an understatement.

And as I finish, Betty Richmond phones and informs me that her stylist has arrived from Washington with several wedding dresses for me to choose from. Would I please meet with them in the Richmonds' suite.

Oh, why not? Let's get this show going.

~ ~ ~

Standing half naked in front of Betty and her gay black English stylist (who'd have thought?!), I strut my stuff, kind of getting off on Betty's obvious embarrassment that I don't wear underwear—well, a tiny thong and that's it.

Raoul, the stylist, gets off on it, too. I can tell he's relishing Betty's embarrassment as much as I am.

"This girl is a young beauty," Raoul announces. "Restless and untamed like the sea. Such a body!"

I step into dress number one. A frilled white concoction, full length and hideous.

"No!" Raoul shrieks. "I have brought all the wrong choices. You did not tell me, Naughty Betty, that we are dressing a wild gypsy with fire in her eyes and a figure to die for!"

I think I love Raoul. He is flamboyant and fabulous with an outrageous proper English accent. How do he and Betty fit? And he calls her Naughty Betty—it's hilarious.

I step out of dress number one and into the next dress.

"No!" Raoul shrieks again, throwing up his hands. "It is not at all right. I will call my people in Washington, they will send more choices. I *know* what this young beauty needs."

Thank goodness there's somebody crazier than me in the room.

Betty looks pained as usual. "When will the new dresses arrive?" she questions. "The wedding is almost upon us."

"Tomorrow, darling," Raoul assures her. "Tomorrow you will see perfection!"

I step out of dress number two. Bad timing, for it is at

this exact moment Peter Richmond enters the room, and here I am with my tits on display.

Big reaction all around.

Betty: "For God's sake, Lucky, cover up!"

Raoul: "Ooops!"

Peter: "Excuse *me*." This said while backing out of the room, but not before getting an eyeful.

Betty throws me a withering look. "Put your clothes on," she hisses.

Yes, ma'am. Or not. What if I feel like strolling around naked?

I grab my T-shirt and slither into my jeans.

"We need some decent clothes for this girl," Betty snaps, fed up with playing nice. "Do you *see* what she looks like? Put together a full wardrobe for her, Raoul. Take her shopping. Here's my Neiman's card."

Raoul winks at me. "We do it, darling. Are you free now?"

"I am."

Raoul is obviously not a man who cares to waste time.

"Then let's go, my wild little gypsy. We have shopping to do."

CHAPTER FORTY-TWO

Neiman's is not on Raoul's hit list for me. "Neiman's is Mrs. Richmond's territory," he informs me with a flick of his wrist. "Chanel, Valentino, designer chic. While *you*, my wild little bird, deserve feathers of another color."

I have found a friend! A very unlikely friend. Mrs. Richmond's personal stylist. A gorgeous gay English black man, with a magnificent ponytail, ebony skin, and skillfully khol-outlined eyes. What the heck is he doing with *her*?

I ask. *Of course* I ask.

Raoul smiles mysteriously. "I am the most sought-after stylist in Washington," he informs me, "so naturally every lady of quality desires my services."

"But—"

He holds up an imperious hand before I can utter another word. "I dress everyone from the first lady to Fantasia Montobella—and in case you are wondering who Fantasia Montobella is, *he* is the premier drag queen in

Washington." Raoul flashes a row of extremely white teeth. "I am—as they say—in demand."

I nod. I get it.

"And you, my wild gypsy, what is your story?"

I give a casual shrug. "I guess I'm getting married."

"You're very young."

"On the outside," I allow.

Raoul does not question me any further. Instead he takes me on a dizzying round of shopping to a series of magical boutiques full of clothes I totally fall in love with.

"How do you know all these places?" I gasp, trying on an amazing filmy chiffon dress.

"It is my job," Raoul replies, standing back, hand on slim hip as he looks me over. "Yes," he decides. "This dress is perfect on you."

I am in awe. Fashion has never been my thing, but then I've never been exposed to the likes of Raoul before, and he has an eye for what suits me. The truth is, he gets me, and I am extraordinarily grateful that somebody does.

After a while we stop for coffee and a chat.

"I do not wish to pry, child," Raoul says. "However, you and Craven . . . why?"

I would love to tell him the truth, but I realize it would be foolish to do so. He works with Mrs. Richmond—who knows if he can keep a secret?

"Well," I say, choosing my words carefully, "I, uh, think that Craven needs someone like me. I might be younger but I'm way wiser."

Raoul rolls his expressive eyes. "True love it's not."

I manage an enigmatic smile. "We'll see," I murmur.

"Indeed we will," Raoul sighs.

~ ~ ~

Later there is dinner with Gino, the Richmonds, myself, and Craven.

Yippee! Fun times!

I wear one of my new outfits picked out by Raoul. Not as traditional as Betty would've preferred, only *I* love it. Loose black pants and a shoestring top. Bold gold hoop earrings and a jangle of bracelets complete the outfit. Even Gino comments, "Lookin' good, kiddo."

A compliment indeed.

Craven stares at me openmouthed. "You're so p . . . pretty," he stammers. Senator Richmond throws me a few lecherous looks, while Mrs. Senator has nothing to say.

Is this my new life? Spending all my time with these people? Because I'm sure that Gino will be on the vanishing list once he's got me safely married off. What a relief it must be for him. No more worries about his errant daughter, she's tucked away in Washington with the Richmonds.

I think about what he's done. He's virtually delivered me to the Richmonds in exchange for not revealing Peter's dalliance with the delectable Ms. Blue. And it's obvious they don't mind *that* much, because who else were they going to unload Craven on? He's not exactly Mister Personality of the Year.

Gino doesn't know it yet, but he owes me big-time. I *will* work alongside him. I *will* be heir to the family business. One of these days it'll happen. Oh yes, Washington is just a stepping stone. A place for me to bide my time.

People keep coming over to our table and congratulating us. The news is out. Apparently so are the wedding invitations, which I haven't even seen. Why would I? I'm only the bride.

Craven sits beside me, a peacock smile on his long thin face. He's such a sad sack that I can't even bring myself to hate him. It's not his fault we're stuck in this circumstance.

I think about our wedding night and shudder. Ugh! Will I really have to do it with him?

I can't imagine. I am convinced that although he's older than me he's totally inexperienced, whereas I—even though I've never gone all the way—have plenty of moves.

Truth is, I'm probably a bit sex-crazy, hormones raging, all that stuff. Girls can want it just as much as boys do, and that doesn't make them sluts. Sex is all about equality— nobody scoring off anyone else, just good healthy sex. It's a given.

I wonder what Marco's like in bed. No doubt awesome. When I pressed my lips against his it was pure heaven. Too bad he's driven me to hate him.

And because I'm thinking about him, naturally he appears, whispers something in Gino's ear, and after excusing himself, Gino goes off with Marco. I wonder what's up. I want to be a part of it. I can solve problems, too.

"Your father is a busy man," Betty remarks, tapping talonlike nails on the tabletop.

Not as busy as Peter, I want to say. The Marabelle Blue pics of him and her having crazy sex are still burned into my mind, probably never to be forgotten.

Dinner concludes without the return of Gino. I wonder where he is. What dire crisis has arisen that he has to deal with.

Once again Craven escorts me to the elevator. Once again I receive a chaste kiss on the cheek.

This is turning into a ritual. At least I have the arrival of Dario to look forward to.

Tomorrow is another day, and I am determined to make the best of it.

CHAPTER FORTY-THREE

I love my brother and, man, he's looking fantastic! Tall and blond and hot! We hug and kiss and dance around the penthouse like a couple of maniacs. He's my family, and I am so thrilled to see him.

When he emerges from his bedroom, Gino acts as if he's pleased, too. He claps Dario on the shoulders and gives him a manly hug. Dario towers over him.

"This is it," Gino says, his voice deep and full of pride. "Your first Vegas trip, Dario. You gotta get into it, kid, gotta learn about the family business, 'cause one day you'll be runnin' the whole shebang. You'll be takin' over from me."

I note the widening of Dario's devastatingly blue eyes.

"Yeah, Dad," he mumbles, because what else *can* he say?

"Marco's gonna show you the setup," Gino continues. "Give you an idea of how we do things around here."

"Can he show me, too?" I pipe up.

Gino shakes his head like he can't really be bothered to reply.

"When you gonna get it into your thick head, Lucky?" he growls. "You're a girl. Girls an' business don't cut it. You're gettin' married into an important family, an' before you know it you'll be poppin' out babies, so quit with the whinin'."

Am I whining? I don't think so. I am merely making a request to receive equal treatment with my brother. Is that too much to ask?

Apparently so, for I've put an annoyed expression on Gino's face.

Screw him. He's on my hate list again. He had someone take sneak photos of his so-called movie-star girlfriend getting down and dirty with the senator. Not nice. Not nice at all.

I keep my cool—fighting with Gino will get me no-where. I just have this huge fear for Dario, because if Gino gets so much as an inkling that Dario is gay . . .

I shudder to think of the consequences.

Before I can launch into a battle with Gino, both Marco and Flora put in an appearance: Marco to take Dario on a tour of the hotel, and Flora to escort me to meet with Betty Richmond and her wedding planner.

Sighing, I go with Flora and her fake boobs, although I would much prefer to be on the hotel tour with Dario.

"See you at lunch," I call out to Dario.

He throws me a slightly panic-stricken look. The last

thing he's interested in is being taught the intricacies of building an enormous hotel and casino, then running it. Dario is no Gino. *I* am. Only Daddy Dearest doesn't seem to get it.

Reluctantly, Dario goes off with Marco—whom I totally ignore. He doesn't deserve so much as a good morning from me. We are over. *Over.*

Sorry, Marco, you had your chance and you blew it.

~ ~ ~

Ah, the wedding planner, a slim, trim, birdlike woman with darting eyes, plumped-up lips, and a bad wig—at least it looks like a wig to me. Her name is Talia Primm, and she is no Raoul.

Flora delivers me and leaves.

Miss Primm is armed with notebooks and charts and samples of various items. She obviously means business, for there is no friendly conversation, just a brusque—"We have to move fast, Lucky, no dillydallying. Decisions must be immediate and final if I'm to pull this off."

Like I care. I don't. I'm not interested in choosing flower arrangements, tablecloths, music, food, the cake. One day, when and if I have a proper wedding—one that means something to me—that's the time I'll get into all the details.

Betty Richmond is not present, she probably has better things to do with her time, like maybe spy on her horny husband.

I wonder if Betty cheats, too. Probably not, who would want her?

After an hour of boring decisions, I tell Miss Primm that she is way more equipped to handle everything than I am, and whatever she decides is fine with me.

She raises a thinly penciled eyebrow, and is it my imagination or does her wig shift slightly?

"Most brides are adamant about what they want," she says. "You don't seem overly concerned."

I shrug. "I'm young," I murmur. "You know better than me what'll work. You're the expert."

Flattery does it every time. Miss Primm gives a tight smile and bobs her head. Once again I'm sure I see her wig shift.

"Very well, Lucky, I will take it upon myself to make sure everything is perfect," she says, clicking her teeth.

"I know you will," I answer, heading for the door.

Flora was due to meet me after two hours with Miss Primm, but since I am out of there early I am free to roam. Something Gino obviously doesn't want me to do.

Is he scared I'll make a run for it?

Probably.

I spend my free hour wandering around the hotel. There is so much to see—a variety of restaurants and coffee shops, a spa, two magnificent swimming pools, a mini golf course, a theater. And, located to the side of the hotel, a bunch of luxury villas reserved for high rollers.

The entire hotel is a wonderland of activity. Then

there's the casino itself, the real moneymaker, where it all happens.

This is where I discover Raoul at a blackjack table, accompanied by a young Asian guy in a smart gray suit.

"Hey," I say, hovering.

"Good morning, gypsy girl," Raoul responds, flashing his whiter-than-white teeth.

Gypsy girl, my new nickname, I love it!

Seeing Raoul lifts my spirits, he has a zest for life that is catching.

"I expect you're wondering when your wedding dress will arrive," he says, indicating to the dealer that he's ready to cash in.

"Only one dress?" I say. "What if I don't like it?"

"Trust me, child," Raoul assures me, pushing his chair away from the table. "You will."

I do trust him—I can't wait to see what he's picked out for me. One thing I'm sure of, it won't be a traditional wedding dress. Raoul has an eye for what I like, or so I hope.

"Is it black?" I ask mischievously. "A Goth wedding dress would suit me fine."

"I'm sure it would," Raoul opines. "And my reputation would therefore be shot to hell."

I giggle.

He smiles.

The young Asian man follows us out of the casino.

"Meet Akio," Raoul says, with a casual wave of his hand. "My partner in love."

I gather they're a couple, not a random pickup as I'd assumed at first sight.

"Why don't you join me and my brother for lunch?" I suggest. "You'll really like Dario, he's special."

I want to add, *And he plays for your team.* Only I don't, because it's up to Dario who he tells and who he doesn't.

Raoul turns to Akio as if *he's* the decision maker, which strikes me as odd since Akio has to be at least fifteen years younger than Raoul.

Akio gives a stiff nod. A man of few words. I hope that Dario doesn't mind me inviting them. It's not just because they're gay that I did so, it's because I like Raoul a lot and I think Dario will, too.

Raoul takes my arm. "And what have *you* been up to, young lady?" he asks.

"Well," I reply, realizing I have nothing exciting to report. "I met with the wedding planner Mrs. Richmond flew in."

Raoul rolls his eyes. "Talia Primm," he says with a weary sigh. "Miss Pain-in-the-Ass, as she's known around town."

I giggle at the way he pronounces "ass." It sounds so proper, said with an English accent.

"Did Miss Primm attempt to boss you around?" he inquires.

"Not really. I simply told her that she could make all the decisions, which seemed to please her."

"Wise child," Raoul says.

And so we proceed to the restaurant.

CHAPTER FORTY-FOUR

I had no idea Dario could cast such a spell, but the moment Raoul meets him there is chemistry in the air. Raoul, a sophisticated and worldly man in his forties, and my teenage beautiful blond brother. Wow! Who would've thought?

Akio is not pleased—he senses it, too, and keeps on shooting Dario dagger-filled glares of meanness.

Dario seems oblivious. He rattles on about school and painting and books he's enjoyed reading, while Raoul—surprisingly silent—drinks in every word.

Does Dario understand the effect he's having?

I doubt it.

The truth is I have no idea how deep Dario is into the gay thing. Maybe it's just a phase. Or maybe not. I'm at a loss.

I need to find out—do gay people take one look at each other and just know?

I am confused; I'm so not up on gay etiquette.

By the time lunch is over I take a deep breath and drag Dario away before Raoul eats him for dessert!

"Your dress will be here later," Raoul calls after me. "Four o'clock in my suite. Bring Dario."

Oh yes, I bet he wants me to bring Dario.

Dario still seems oblivious to the fact that Raoul was fawning all over him.

I throw my brother a penetrating look. "Are you still gay?" I ask as we make our way back to the penthouse.

He seems perplexed. "What?" he says.

"Gay? You?" I persist.

"It's not like measles," he says with an irritated scowl. "It doesn't just come and go."

"Well, Raoul's in love," I state, which causes Dario to burst into a fit of hysterical laughter.

I stare at him, thinking how like my mom he looks with his blazing blue eyes and shock of blond hair. I wonder if Gino sees the resemblance. Then there's me—a female version of my dad with the same jet-black hair and intense dark eyes. I bet Gino wishes it was the other way around.

"How was the tour of the hotel?" I ask Dario, thinking a change of subject might be in order.

"Hardly my scene," he replies. "I'm not interested, Lucky, you know that."

"Yes, I do know. And what really pisses me off is that Gino doesn't see it. I'm all ready to jump aboard and you're a total nonstarter. It's so not fair."

"Yeah," Dario agrees as we get in the elevator. "It sucks."

"One of these days he'll get it," I say, full of confidence. "You'll see."

"I'm sure." Dario hesitates for a second, then plunges on. "I'm gonna ask him if I can go to art school in San Francisco."

"You are?"

"What do you think he'll say?"

"I think you'd better pick your moment. You know Gino, totally unpredictable. Who knows *what* his reaction will be."

We enter the penthouse and both flop onto one of the luxurious overstuffed couches in the living room.

"So," Dario says, scrutinizing my face. "I can't believe you're getting married."

"Better than another dumb school," I say flippantly.

"You're sure about that?" he asks, watching me closely. "Who's this Craven dude, anyway?"

"His dad is a senator, his mom is into the whole charity bit."

"I'm asking about him, not his family."

"He's . . . uh . . . kind of . . . uh . . . boring."

"I don't get it," Dario says, hauling his butt off the couch and going behind the bar to get a Coke.

"Nobody said you had to," I argue.

"C'mon, Lucky, why are you doing this?" Dario demands, opening the can.

"It's difficult to explain."

Dario screws up his eyes. "No shit?"

"Look," I say firmly. "I've got to get away from being under Gino's control. If I marry Craven I won't be regarded as a dumb little kid anymore. I'll be my own person, an adult."

"You'll be somebody's *wife*."

"Don't worry," I say, getting all defensive. "I've thought it through, I know exactly what I'm doing."

"You're just like Gino—stubborn."

I contemplate whether I should tell Dario about the blackmail pics, then I decide not to.

"It's okay," I say soothingly. "This is gonna work out for me, you'll see. In fact, little bro—you can bet on it."

~ ~ ~

My wedding dress couldn't be more perfect. Short in front, long in the back—a soft flowing material covered in tiny sparkling beads. Not traditional at all, it has a kind of hippie vibe.

Raoul stands back and surveys me with a pleased expression. "Such a fit in every way," he murmurs. "You are a beauty—a dark wild colt of a beauty."

"I love it!" I purr. "How did you know?"

Raoul nods to himself. "Some things are meant to be, child. This dress was waiting for you."

Mrs. Richmond is nowhere to be seen. I couldn't care less whether she approves the dress or not because it's what I'm wearing.

"Where is your brother?" Raoul asks. "Such a delightful young man."

"Uh . . . Gino grabbed him—he's all about teaching him the hotel business."

"Surely that is not where Dario's interests lie?"

"I guess not, but my dad can be very . . . uh . . . forceful."

"Dario is an old soul, a gentle boy."

I nod. I have a hunch that Raoul knows. I just hope to God Gino doesn't find out.

"Are you aware that Peter Richmond is planning a bachelor night for Craven?" Raoul asks. "I thought that you might allow me the honor of arranging a similar evening for you."

Wow! Haven't thought about celebrating the birth of my new life! And who would I celebrate with anyway? I don't have any friends here.

"Who would you invite?" I ask.

"Whomever you like," Raoul replies.

"*Not* Mrs. Richmond," I say firmly.

"It will be our secret," Raoul assures me. "There are many amusing people I know here in Vegas. Let's say it will be a different kind of evening. Oh yes, and be sure to bring Dario. I know he'll enjoy it."

And I understand exactly why Raoul has it in mind to entertain us.

CHAPTER FORTY-FIVE

Miss Drew arrives from L.A. at the same time as groups of wedding guests begin to fly in. The guests include Gino's friends and business acquaintances from L.A. and New York, Washington dignitaries, and Betty Richmond's tribe of female friends, a frightening group of women with helmet hair and painstaking expressions. Betty throws a lunch for me, which is my idea of hell on earth. The women gawk at me as if I'm a strange creature from outer space. Not to be intimidated, I stare right back at them.

Everyone thinks I'm pregnant. Why else would this rushed wedding be happening?

And then a huge surprise takes place, one that Gino has omitted to tell me. The Stanislopouloses arrive, Dimitri and Olympia.

When did Gino and Dimitri become so close that Gino invited them to my wedding? I can only assume that they bonded on their quest to track down me and Olympia in the South of France. Talk about a shocking turn of events. I haven't seen or spoken to Olympia since we were discovered hiding out at her aunt's villa. Her last words accused me of telling Gino and Dimitri where to find us. Untrue and hurtful.

Now here she is in Vegas, all blonde and bouncing curls, bountiful bosoms and with a huge smile on her face.

She envelops me in a best-friend hug and whispers in my ear, "You sly piece of work—grabbing yourself a senator's son! Congrats, girl. I wish *I* was getting married."

Apparently the past is the past and all is forgiven.

Truth is, I am kind of delighted to see her. We shared so many adventures, and without Warris the Sleaze around, she is just like the old Olympia I used to know and bond with.

"What are you *doing* here?" I ask. "I had no clue you were coming."

"Daddy's into gambling," Olympia explains. "His latest girlfriend's never been to Vegas, so when the invite arrived he decided we should make the trip. Gives him an excuse to use his plane."

"Wow! It's really fab to see you."

Olympia gives me another close hug. She smells of a very expensive perfume and her diamond ear studs are way bigger than mine.

"Little Lucky Saint, all grown up," she exclaims, checking me out. "I love it! Does your fiancé have any hot friends?"

I choke back laughter. As if.

"I haven't met his friends yet," I say. "When I do, I'll let you know."

Olympia licks her jammy lips and leans in for a quick whisper. "Are you knocked up?"

I shake my head. *No, Olympia, unlike you, I am still a virgin. Although much experienced in other areas involving sex.*

"No way," I answer with a vigorous shake of my head.

"Well, I have to say you're lookin' awesome. This dude must be giving you all the right moves in bed."

Ah . . . if she only knew.

"When do I get to meet him?" Olympia demands. "I promise I won't steal him from you, not unless you want me to. Although you do know that I'm quite irresistible to the male sex."

She giggles as if she's making a joke, but I know her all too well; she truly believes she can get any man she goes after, and 95 percent of the time she's right.

"I guess you've forgotten all about Warris?" I question.

"Who?" Olympia says, straight-faced.

A beat, then we both burst out laughing.

"You have to admit we had fun," Olympia insists.

I remember Jon and nod my head. Better to dwell on the positive rather than remember all the negative things that happened.

"So," I say. "Betty Richmond is desperado to meet your dad."

"Why is that?"

"Could be 'cause he's a billionaire with a plane and an island."

"She sounds lovely."

"Anyway, Gino's spoken to Dimitri, and we're all supposed to meet for dinner tonight."

"Cool," Olympia says, fluffing out her hair. "That means you'll get an eyeful of Daddy's fuck-friend. She's Russian, six feet tall, and a bitch on wheels."

Perfect, I think, *we should sit her next to Peter Richmond and watch the sparks ignite.*

Olympia links her arm through mine. "Amaze hotel," she raves. "We should go to the spa, I haven't had a manicure in three days. I'm dying to tell you about my latest. He's a German and bisexual. He gives going underground a whole new meaning."

Ah, Olympia is definitely back.

~ ~ ~

Two hours later I am exhausted. Listening to Olympia's sexual highjinks is like a nonstop sex marathon. Details, details, details. Too many details!

Fortunately she is too busy talking about herself to question me.

I am relieved, 'cause I have nothing to reveal. Horny Jeff doesn't count. I need a real session of "almost" before marriage swallows me up.

Can girls feel horny?

You bet they can.

Maybe with Olympia in town I will be able to slip out after dinner. I plot and plan with Dario, who still hasn't gotten up the nerve to broach the subject of art school with Gino.

"We should go to a club when dinner's through," I suggest. "Somewhere we can let loose. I'm starting to feel majorly trapped."

Dario doesn't seem too enthusiastic. He's confessed to me that he misses his teacher boyfriend, Eric, and wishes he was here.

I do not wish to come across as a prude—however, isn't it kind of inappropriate for a teacher to be sleeping with a student? Especially when that student is my baby brother. I mean, I've met Eric and everything, and he seems like a cool guy. But still . . .

Soon Olympia will meet Craven, and I can't help wondering what she'll think of him. She'll immediately get that it's all a sham. As well as I know her, that's how well she knows me.

Too bad. I've come this far, I'm not backing down now. Besides, I think Gino would kill me if I did.

I have faced the fact that Gino has deals to make, connections to cement. And the Washington connection is a big one for him. It wouldn't be cool for me to blow it. Besides, maybe the Washington connection will be *my* key to the future. Why not? Nothing is impossible.

~ ~ ~

Dario is into getting stoned. He has a bag of pot with him—courtesy of teacher Eric—and he thinks we should roll joints and smoke it before the big dinner.

I kind of don't want to, 'cause I prefer to remain clear-headed at all times. But Dario insists, and as a supportive sister I finally agree.

He's already met Craven, they played tennis in the morning. "C'mon, Lucky. The dude's a total jerk," he'd told me, as if I didn't already know. "He's got no personality, all he seems to do is boast about his mom and how fantastic she is."

"There's more to this upcoming marriage than you know," I'd informed him. "Trust me, I understand exactly what I'm letting myself in for."

Dario had shaken his head and muttered something about me being a fool.

Maybe I am. However, I truly think I know what I'm doing.

We share a joint out on the terrace of the penthouse lest Gino come sniffing around. I have to admit, it *is* relaxing.

Olympia calls to find out what I'm wearing.

"Black," I say. "I'm into my Goth cycle."

"I'm wearing Dolce," she informs me. "Pink. I plan to outshine everyone, including Daddy's Russian bitch."

Ah, Olympia, modest as ever.

Soon it's time to leave for dinner at the Lake restaurant. There are numerous restaurants in the hotel—each one more luxurious than the last. The Lake is Gino's particular favorite as it overlooks a series of cascading waterfalls and a man-made lake, very glam.

Gino emerges from his dressing room clad all in black, his gangsterish look.

We go together nicely. Father and daughter. A perfect matching pair.

"My children," he says, beaming at both of us. "The two of you certainly make a man proud."

And with these words ringing in my ears we set off for dinner.

CHAPTER FORTY-SIX

The Russian bitch—as Olympia refers to her father's girl-friend—is over six feet tall and a supermodel. She has skin as smooth as white ivory, slanted green eyes, and a slender body to die for. She speaks very little English, and every man in the place is salivating over her. Dimitri greets me with a bearlike hug, making no mention of the South of France debacle, then after the hug—which goes on a tad long—he introduces me to his girlfriend, Tasha. I think I've seen her on the cover of *Sports Illustrated* or one of those magazines where women appear unreal. Tasha looks unreal *and* untouchable. A double whammy. It's not a sexy vibe, and I wonder why all the men are drooling.

Gino is definitely turning on the charm, so is Peter Rich-mond. Craven seems to be terrified.

I want to laugh—men are so predictable. They either drool or they run.

Olympia makes her entrance: She resembles a pink

cupcake in her over-the-top dress, with boobs spilling out. She flirts outrageously with Craven, who manages to cower away, looking even more petrified.

Betty has her usual bad-smell-under-the-nose expression. Dario is definitely stoned. And Aunt Jen and Uncle Costa have joined the party. Then there's Alison, Craven's uptight sister with swept-up hair and a morose expression. It's a lively group.

I wonder why Gino doesn't have a date—surely Gino the Ram should be covered in women? I guess he wants to get through the wedding and then he'll take off once I'm safely shipped to Washington.

"Lucky," Dimitri says, one hand on his girlfriend's thigh under the table, which I can't help but notice. "This is a wonderful time for you. A big celebration."

It is?

"Uh . . . yes," I agree.

"I offered you and your intended a honeymoon on my island," Dimitri continues. "However, I understand you will be heading to the Bahamas."

"We are," I say.

"The O . . . Ocean Club," Craven stammers. "Mother recommended it, she's stayed many times."

"Oh," Olympia drawls sarcastically. "Will *Mother* be going with you?"

Hmm . . . it doesn't take Olympia long to get a bead on Craven and his mother fixation.

"Sadly no," Betty says, concentrating her attention on

Dimitri. "Your island sounds divine—Peter and I are always searching for a new vacation spot."

"Search no more, my lady," Dimitri responds. "You and the senator are welcome to my island as my guests at any time."

And I note his hand traveling farther up his girlfriend's thigh to under her ultrashort dress.

I bet she's not wearing panties.

Tasha's exquisite ivory face remains impassive. She is obviously used to being worshipped or felt up. One or the other.

Olympia has decided to zero in on Peter Richmond. She recognizes a letch when she sees one.

Aunt Jen smiles comfortingly at me. A warm smile. A smile that indicates all is well because sixteen-year-old me is getting her naughty little ass married off to an important political family.

I know for sure that if my mom was still alive this would never be happening.

Gino is in deep conversation with Uncle Costa. Business rules.

Dario is sitting back, stoned, and wishing he was somewhere else.

Everyone seems to have found their comfort zone. Everyone except me.

Olympia leans across the table to say something, her large bosoms almost falling out of her dress.

"When can we get out of here and go have some fun?"

she whispers. "And by the way, your little bro is a real hottie. What's *his* story?"

Ah, Olympia . . . she's never picky. A teenage boy or an old senator. She'll flirt with them all equally.

"Soon," I mouth, thinking, *The sooner the better.*

I have a plan. With Olympia here it will be easy for me to ditch Craven and take off with her. No going back to the penthouse with a stern guard stationed outside. I will be spending the night with my best friend. Who can possibly argue with that?

Gino might, because he knows our history. But Betty has abandoned Dimitri, and now has Gino deep in conversation. I bet it won't be long before he makes an excuse and takes off before the dinner ends.

Yes! It happens exactly as I predicted. Marco appears, mutters in Gino's ear, and Gino gets up. I realize that clearly this is a routine Gino has worked out with Marco to allow him a convenient exit strategy.

Business calls. Good-bye, Daddy Dearest.

"Who the *freak* is *that*?" Olympia asks, staring at Marco as he extracts Gino.

"*That* is Marco," I reply, adding a silent *My Marco, so hands off.*

"Oh," Olympia sighs. "*Now* I get it."

Naturally I'd gone on and on about Marco when we were at L'Evier together. I'm sure I'd spoken about my crush many times. Too many, perhaps.

"Why aren't you marrying *him*?" Olympia demands. "He's gorgeous."

Why indeed, I ask myself.

~ ~ ~

Olympia makes everything easy. I forgot how adept she is at insisting things go her way. Since Dimitri is heading for the gaming tables with Tasha, she commandeers his limousine and driver, and instructs the driver to take us to the most popular club in Vegas. The us is me, her, and Dario.

We make a daring escape after I inform Craven I have to spend some alone-time with my best friend who's flown all the way from Greece to attend our wedding. Actually she was in New York with her mother, but Craven doesn't know that. He is disappointed, but assures me that he understands.

At least he's not difficult, that's one point in his favor.

The club we arrive at is perfect. Loud music blasting in our ears. Flashing lights alerting our senses. And before we know it, we are getting a round of tequila shots from the manager—a man Olympia immediately bonds with.

It amazes me how, at seventeen, she always gets her own way. Nobody checks us for IDs, we are just automatically in—including Dario, who's still only fifteen.

I take big gulps of club air. Intoxicating! Exactly what I need.

Dario and I hit the crowded dance floor and go crazy. I have so much energy to release. Olympia is way busy with the manager—a smooth talker, but not half as smooth as she is. He's met a girl who is not in awe of him simply because he fronts the most popular club in town, and he's way into her. Olympia—well, who knows with Olympia.

And then I see him. Marco. Only he's not *my* Marco anymore. He's sitting in a booth with a girl who is draping herself all over him. And it's not some random girl, it's Flora, my sometime escort, the thirty-something VIP hostess with the dyed red hair and fake boobs.

Oh . . . my . . . God.

For a moment I am frozen to the spot.

Flora.

Really?

Seriously?

They haven't seen me. I am invisible to them because they are too busy tonguing each other to death.

I hate them both.

A plan. I need a plan of action.

And then it comes to me . . .

CHAPTER FORTY-SEVEN

"Hey—Marco, Flora—fancy running into you here," I say in a prepared and cool fashion. Marco glances up and looks quite startled to see me. "Lucky," he mumbles. "What the hell are *you* doin' here?"

I can tell he's had a few drinks too many.

"Enjoying myself, just like you."

"Jesus Christ!" he steams. "You shouldn't be here."

Flora reaches into her purse, flips out a lipstick, and proceeds to plaster it on her lips.

"Are you going to run and report me to Gino?" I ask, making direct eye contact with the ex–love of my life.

He shakes his head as if he doesn't know *what* he's about to do.

"It really makes no difference now, does it?" I say. "The train has left the station. I'll be a married woman in a couple days, so really I can do whatever I want, right?"

"You shouldn't be here," Marco mutters, repeating

himself. "You shouldn't be in this club drinkin', you're underage."

"Not too young to get married though," I say with a scathing look. "Not too underage for that."

Flora jumps to her feet. I can tell that she doesn't want to be involved in this confrontation. I am her boss's daughter and she's scared of this somehow reflecting badly on her.

"Going to the little girls' room," she trills, and scampers off, leaving me alone with the Betrayer.

Marco gives me a long serious look. His dark hair is rumpled and I notice he is unshaven. It only adds to his attractiveness. Crap! If only he wasn't so impossibly handsome.

"Y'know, Lucky," he says at last, "I was only lookin' out for you."

"Thanks," I answer. "But believe me, Marco, I am all grown up, I can look out for myself—I don't need any help."

"Yeah," he says slowly. "I'm beginning to realize that."

Really, Marco? I am slightly thrown off balance by his choice of words. Is he finally acknowledging my grown-up status?

"Uh . . . well . . . um . . . good," I mutter.

Do I sound like a total moron?

Yes, I think I do.

"I'm sorry I tried to kiss you," I say, thinking it might be time to put our relationship—such as it is—back on track. "I know it was totally inappropriate and that you didn't want it."

"Lucky," he says, leaning back and giving me a long soulful look—a look that makes my heart melt. "It wasn't that I didn't *want* it, the problem is you're so goddamn beautiful. But you're too young for me, Lucky, and I work for Gino. An' those are two things I can't do anything about."

Oh . . . my . . . God! I am about to have a total collapse. Did I just hear right? Is this Marco telling me he *wanted* me to kiss him? *Am I dreaming?*

Before I can find out, my clever plan zooms into action. Olympia, club manager, and some other random dude Olympia has recruited at my request descend on me. And random dude acts all cozy, as if we're a couple! Olympia has told him to do exactly that.

Yes, this is my clever plan to make Marco jealous. Too bad, because now all I want to do is sit down next to him, fall into his deep, dark, somewhat drunken gaze, and hear what else he has to say.

I love him. I do! I really do!

Then Flora returns to the table and the spell is totally broken.

Marco puts a finger to his lips. "Code of silence," he says with a wry smile. "This time I won't be running to Gino. That's a promise."

"Thanks," I mumble in a strained voice, before random dude pulls me out onto the dance floor.

I am dazed and confused. What is going on? Why am I light-headed and filled with joy?

Should I call off my wedding and wait for Marco?

Inner voice to the rescue. *Don't be a ditz. He didn't declare his undying love, he simply said he didn't mind you kissing him.*

Oh, crap! Once again I am so confused.

Random dude pulls me close. "I'm Luke," he says.

Like I care.

"Glad I could be of assistance."

I bet you are.

"That old dude looked pissed when I dragged you away."

"He's not so old," I mutter, quite insulted.

"Well, he did look pissed. But you wanted me to rescue you, right? That's what your friend said."

Oh, Olympia, thanks for all your help, only unfortunately your timing was way off. Now I'll never know what Marco was going to say next.

Later the four of us—Olympia, club manager, Luke, and me—go back to the the club manager's apartment overlooking the Strip, because Olympia insists that I return the favor she did for me. Dario is long gone—he took the limo back to the hotel, or at least I hope that's what he did. I do not relish the idea of baby bro trolling around Vegas searching out gay action.

Ah yes, it's the same old Olympia, thinking only of herself, 'cause I have no intention of getting it on with Luke. First off he's not my type, and second my thoughts are crammed full of Marco.

Drinks are offered and it doesn't take long before Olympia and club manager vanish into his bedroom, leaving me alone with Luke. He has brown spiky hair, a stocky build, and an expectant look on his face.

Well, if he's expecting anything from me, he's way out of luck. I am *so* not in the mood for "almost."

He makes a lame attempt to kiss me, and when I resist, he produces a vial of cocaine and starts laying out lines on the coffee table.

Awkward! The whole scenario is totally awkward.

"Coke isn't my deal," I tell him, backing away.

"C'*mon*," he counters persuasively. "It's everyone's deal."

"I'm getting married."

"That's why y'should be making the most of your freedom."

"You're right," I say quickly. "And that's why I'm heading to my hotel. Tell Olympia I'll send the car back for her."

To Luke's credit he lets me leave without giving me a hard time.

Back at the hotel I check in on Dario. He's safely in his bed, asleep.

I hear noises coming from Gino's bedroom, so I edge toward the door, curious as to who he's with now. It seems Daddy Dearest doesn't have a particular type.

I can hear a woman groaning in the throes of ecstasy. It makes me shiver—I shouldn't be spying on my father, it's none of my business. Somehow I can't help myself.

Sex over, there is now conversation taking place.

I lean closer to the door and, maybe I'm imagining it, but the woman sounds awfully like Betty Richmond—my future mother-in-law.

No. Impossible.

Or is it?

CHAPTER FORTY-EIGHT

It's morning, and I am lying in bed contemplating the situation, such as it is. Daddy Dearest is sleeping with Betty Richmond—my future mother-in-law. And I know this for a fact, because after hearing what I thought was her voice I stayed up and spied—watching her leave on one of the security cameras Gino has set up.

Holy crap! My father is doing the dirty with Mrs. Dead Eyes. *Ugh!* It's *so* not right.

And I have questions. Does the senator know? Does Craven?

I think not.

Oh my God, it's so screwed up. And yet it makes sense. It all fits into the arranged-marriage situation.

Knowledge is power. And now I have it. If I wanted to, I could go to Gino and tell him that I know everything and that I refuse to marry Craven.

Then what?

No. I will go ahead, marry Craven, forge my own iden-tity, get a divorce, then I'll confront Gino and tell him exactly what I want. A full stake in the family business, a position of importance. I want to be Gino's partner.

Dario hops into my room, interrupting my reverie of thought.

"You're not up," he says.

"That's pretty obvious," I answer.

"Well, get your lazy butt up."

"Why should I?"

"'Cause Gino is insisting I go with him to a brunch with the Richmonds, an' I'm not doin' it without you."

"For crap's sake," I grumble, "you go, I don't have to."

"Yes, you do," Dario insists. "They're gonna be *your* family, not mine. So there's no reason *I* should get stuck."

He has a point, my blond and beautiful gay brother.

"Okay," I say with a reluctant sigh. "Give me five, I'll throw on some clothes."

I jump out of bed, while Dario plops himself down on top of the covers.

"What happened after I left last night?" he asks.

"Exactly nothing," I respond, pulling on my jeans.

"You're such a slut," he says with a sly grin.

"What?"

"Going off with those two sleazeballs."

"I didn't go off with anyone, Olympia did."

"Yeah, *sure*," Dario says disbelievingly.

"Oh, shut *up*."

"Why should I?"

I decide ignoring him is the way to go as I finish dressing.

I can't wait to see how Gino acts in front of dear old Betty. It promises to be most entertaining.

~ ~ ~

Betty Richmond is in her tennis outfit. A short white pleated skirt and a sensible sleeveless top. Her skin is leather-tanned and taut; the muscles in her upper arms appear manly and strong. Not exactly a sex goddess. I wonder what Gino can possibly see in her.

"Good morning, dear," she greets me.

Good morning, you cheating whore, I want to say. Instead I give her a wan smile.

Peter Richmond winks at me. "Only two more days," he says. "Are you excited?"

Is he kidding? Excited. About *what*?

Craven comes loping in, red-faced and out of breath. "S . . . sorry I'm late," he stammers.

"*Why* are you late?" Betty demands.

"I w . . . was on the phone."

"With whom?" Betty asks, dead eyes requiring an immediate answer.

Is she serious? I feel sorry for Craven that he has to deal with such a controlling bitch of a mother. He's twenty-one years old. What business of hers is it *who* he's talking to? I decide that I'd better teach him to grow some balls, he needs them desperately.

"Andrew actually," Craven says. "He's n . . . not going to be able to make it in time for the wedding."

"Well, that's extremely inconvenient," Betty snaps.

Craven hangs his head and looks mortified.

Realizing everyone at the table is listening, Betty decides to mortify Craven even more and explain. "Andrew was supposed to be Craven's best man," she says with a waspish grimace. "They went to college together, but it's obviously not important enough for Andrew to put himself out. Craven is not a priority."

"Hey," Gino says. "These things happen."

"Unfortunately they always seem to happen to Craven," Betty says, as if it's *his* fault.

"Got an idea," Gino offers. "Dario's here—*he'll* be Craven's best man."

I sneak a quick glance at Dario. He looks horrified.

"That would be wonderful," Betty exclaims, shifting her dead eyes toward Dario. "And such a handsome young man, too."

And so it is arranged. The Santangelos are an all-giving family. A bride and a best man all wrapped up in one neat little package. How very nice.

~ ~ ~

After brunch Dario and I take off and meet up with Olympia. True to herself she is all dreamy-eyed and postcoital.

"I think I'm going to move to Vegas," she sighs as we all loll out by one of the luxurious hotel swimming pools.

"You're crazy," I say, because the truth is that Olympia *is* a little bit crazy.

"Oh, yes," Olympia responds, adjusting her bikini top so that her full cleavage is on display. "*I'm* crazy, and *you're* the one getting married at sixteen."

"Why d'you want to move to Vegas?" I ask.

"'Cause Rick thinks I should."

"Who's Rick?"

"The club manager, idiot. We're in love."

"Lust," I correct.

"What?"

"One night of lust and you're anyone's."

"Thanks. What makes you think this isn't the real thing?"

"'Cause you've only known him for one day."

"And how long have *you* known Craven?"

"Different situation," I point out. "Anyway, I'd like to see Dimitri's face if you told him you were moving to Vegas."

"You're both freakin' nuts," Dario says, joining in. "And now I've got to go get fitted for some dumb dinner jacket 'cause of you." He gives me a brotherly glare and stands up. Girls in the vicinity all crane to get a better look at his blond six-foot frame in blue swim shorts that match his eyes.

"Bye-bye, hot baby brother," Olympia singsongs. "If you were only of legal age I'd be all over you."

Dario gives an embarrassed grin. "Good luck with that moving to Vegas thing," he says before taking off.

"He's so wicked cute," Olympia sighs, a mischievous gleam in her eyes. "Does he have a girlfriend?"

"Not that I know of," I reply, hardly about to reveal Dario's secret to Olympia. She has a big mouth and is not good at keeping secrets.

"How come you took off last night?" Olympia asks. "Didn't you like Luke? I thought he was major cute."

"I'm about to get married," I remind her.

"Ah yes, you should be making the most of your freedom."

"That's what Luke said before I ran out on him."

"Then why *did* you leave?"

I left because of Marco. He's on my mind big-time.

I left because I truly, deeply love him.

"'Cause . . . I dunno," I mumble vaguely.

Olympia screws up her eyes. "Are you *sure* you should be doing this? It's not as if you're ecstatically happy."

I nod my head. "It's what I want," I say firmly. "And I'm not about to change my mind."

CHAPTER FORTY-NINE

Marco, Marco, Marco. Wherefore art thou, Marco?

Is Marco all I can think about? The way he moves, his dark eyes, his strong athletic body, his jet-black hair.

Our children would be a combination of both of us. How amazing would *that* be.

Thank goodness there is a Raoul in my life. At least there is someone who can take my mind off my one true love. Raoul is organizing an off-the-grid bachelorette party for me—a party that will take place after the formal "all girls" dinner Betty Richmond has arranged.

"All girls" my ass, Betty and her tribe of uptight friends. Thank goodness there is an Olympia in my life, too.

This is all taking place on the same night as Craven's bachelor party, a party Dario is being forced to attend, since he is now officially Craven's best man. I've told my brother that the moment he can get away he should hop a cab and come join Raoul's event. He's down with that.

Meanwhile there are only two days left before the wedding. Two more long days, and everything is set. I had to sit through an endlessly boring meeting with Talia Primm, who insisted on going over every detail with me so I could approve all her hard work.

"It hasn't been easy putting this all together in such a short period of time," she'd informed me, waiting for me to praise her valiant efforts. "I am a perfectionist, which I am sure you appreciate, and so is Mrs. Richmond."

I rallied, deciding that I may as well make her feel good about herself.

"You've done an awesome job," I assured her.

"Thank you," she'd replied, adjusting her wig.

It seems I am having a pink wedding. Pink tablecloths and napkins; pink place mats; pink flowers. Surely it's Olympia who should be getting married surrounded by her favorite color? It's *so* not me. When the time comes and I have a real wedding, I want it to be black and silver all the way. Me and Marco. Black and silver. And maybe we'll have the ceremony in Bali, or some other exotic location.

Craven is driving me nuts, and I know it's mean of me, but I can't help going out of my way to avoid him. He's so freaking *needy*. It's a total turnoff.

"I h . . . hope they don't have s . . . strippers at my bachelor night," he confides to me.

Is he kidding? Knowing Gino and Dimitri and Peter Richmond, it'll be stripper city.

"Everything will be cool," I tell him. "All you've got to do is relax, sit back, and enjoy yourself."

Oh my God! If he's scared of strippers at his bachelor party, how's he going to behave on our wedding night? I shudder to think. I'm sixteen, and he's way more inexperienced than me. Gulp! Am I going to have to show *him* what to do? This isn't right.

Meanwhile, once I make it through Betty Richmond's dinner, it's about to be all fun ahead.

~ ~ ~

Olympia is outrageous, shocking, and a pure jolt of fresh air. She takes over Betty's dinner, scandalizing the ladies with torrid tales of Dimitri's conquests. "I have no idea how I ended up so normal," she purrs, fluffing out her blonde hair. "With a father like mine I should be a raving nympho."

The ladies gasp in shock, although it's apparent they are eating up every salacious word. They all know who Dimitri Stanislopoulos is. The Greek billionaire shipping tycoon with the reputation of being a rabid ladies' man.

What would I do if Olympia wasn't here?

How would I manage?

Thanks, Olympia, for taking the heat off me.

Dinner ends early, and the two of us hurry upstairs to change into more suitable outfits for Raoul's festivities.

That afternoon we'd gone shopping and both picked out killer outfits. I went totally over the top and chose a tight black leather dress, thigh-high boots, and a to-die-for studded motorcycle jacket. Olympia preferred to take the hooker route, and she ended up getting a shorter-than-short white cleavage-city dress, a silver sequinned shrug, and sky-high heels. "It's Vegas, baby," she'd squealed. "We've gotta go for it!"

We change into our new clothes in Olympia's suite and race from the hotel on our way to Raoul's event.

I am psyched—I don't know what he has planned, but knowing Raoul, it will be something major exciting.

~ ~ ~

Half-naked little people; bikini-clad models of both sexes cavorting in cages; disco balls galore; male strippers; a singing drag queen; and the best music ever!

Yes, Raoul has pulled out all the stops for an over-the-top night of scintillating decadence! Of course, the first question out of his mouth is "Where is your sweet brother?"

Probably shying away in horror from a gaggle of strippers, I think.

"Oh, he'll be here soon," I say.

Raoul smiles, and gestures at the dazzling activities taking place. "You like?"

"We *love!*" Olympia answers for me. "Can I try dancing in a cage? I've always wanted to."

Ah, Olympia, up for any challenge.

And so the evening *really* begins . . .

~ ~ ~

It's late, I have no clue how late. I only know I am totally drunk on endless tequila shots, and that's *so* not me. I'm the girl who likes to stay on top of things, be aware, know what's going on. But I'm allowed to freak out once in a while, aren't I? I'm allowed to get crazy, considering what my future holds.

Dario showed up earlier with gross stories of nude lap dances, and Peter Richmond making a spectacle of himself.

Who cares?

I don't.

I have other things to consider. Where is Marco? Will I see him before my execution—uh, sorry—I mean wedding.

Am I doing the right thing?

I feel sick, make it to the ladies' room, throw up, feel better.

My baby brother insists on taking me back to the hotel. I allow him to lead me from the club even though the mayhem is far from over. I see Olympia making out with one of the male strippers, while Raoul is parading around in full makeup and a long blonde wig.

It's all too much.

I've had fun, but it's time to get serious.

CHAPTER FIFTY

It's morning, I open one eye and I'm shocked to see Gino standing over my bed staring down at me with a pensive expression. Why is he here? Did I do something terrible last night? Something I can't recall?

Memories are a blur. I have a raging headache and I am desperate to pee.

"Daddy," I croak. "What's up?"

"Hey, kiddo," he says, rubbing his hands together. "It's noon. Why're you still sleeping?"

To avoid waking up, I want to say, but I don't.

"Didn't realize it was so late," I mumble.

"How was your dinner with Betty?" he asks.

"Uh . . . fine."

Gino sits himself down on the edge of my bed. I squirm uncomfortably. I feel trapped and certainly not prepared for a cozy father-daughter chat.

"I know Betty's not exactly a mother figure," Gino says, clearing his throat. "But you gotta give her a chance, she's really a good woman."

Good in bed, Daddy? Is that it?

"Okay," I say carefully, wishing he'd leave already.

"I know this is like a big rushed deal," Gino says. "However, one of these days you're gonna thank me. You're gonna tell me I did the right thing."

"If you say so," I manage.

"Yeah, kiddo, I say so." A long beat. "You got no mother—all you got is me an' Dario, an' that's not enough. You need a family around you, an' the Richmonds are just that, a real close family unit."

What is he, blind?

"They're powerful, too," Gino continues. "Well respected, an' well liked. You never know, one day Peter could be sittin' in the White House, with you an' Craven right alongside him."

Yeah, and horses will fly.

"It's okay, Gino," I say. "I get it. I'm cool with the situation."

He gives a sigh of relief. "That's what I wanted to hear, 'cause you know I love you, kiddo. You'll always be my little princess."

My eyes automatically fill with tears. Daddy Dearest certainly knows how to pull my strings.

He gets up. "Tonight," he says, "a quiet dinner. You, me, and Dario."

I nod, he's gone, and so my day begins.

Later Olympia, Dario, and I take up our usual positions beside the pool and rehash last night's activities.

Apparently Dimitri and Tasha ended up having a steaming row after she accused him of sleeping with one of the strippers at Craven's bachelor party.

"The Russian bitch has left the building," Olympia announces, a triumphant gleam in her eyes. "Dimitri doesn't seem to be too concerned."

"Did you tell him you're thinking of moving to Vegas?" I ask.

"Huh?" Olympia manages a look of sheer puzzlement. "What *are* you talking about? Three days and I'm over this place."

I guess club manager Rick is just a distant memory.

Dario reveals more about the bachelor party. "It was my worst nightmare," he says with a shudder. "All those horrible naked girls crawling all over everyone. Gross!"

"Was Marco there?" I ask, suddenly breathless.

"Yeah, he was there."

The image of Marco with naked strippers infuriates me. Surely he doesn't enjoy that kind of thing? Then I think, *Who am I kidding—he's a man, isn't he?*

I have no desire to obsess about Marco anymore. I need to file him away in the back of my head until I'm ready to take his breath away. Because one day it will happen, I have never been more sure of anything. Marco and I are destined to be together. It's a given.

"I adore Raoul," Olympia exclaims. "What a character! Where did you find him?"

"I didn't find him. Betty Richmond did."

"Well, there's a mismatched pair," Olympia drawls. "The uptight hag and the raging queen."

I can't help giggling. I turn to Dario. "What do *you* think of Raoul?"

Dario blushes a deep beet red, and I realize that something must've gone on between them that I don't know about.

Oh dear, Dario's so young and yet not so innocent. Exactly like me.

Olympia's listening, so I think it's best to quickly move on. I jump up. "Last one in the pool is a chicken," I say, making a running dive into the water.

Dario follows me. Olympia doesn't, swimming's not her forte—balancing a margarita and admiring glances from men is.

"So what's up with you and Raoul?" I ask, surfacing with a sputter.

"How'd you know?" Dario questions, treading water.

"It's not like you have a poker face."

"Nothing major. He's nice, he makes me laugh."

"*And* he's got a boyfriend."

"So've I."

"Okay, then. I guess you know what you're doing."

Dario suddenly grins, and I realize he does know what he's doing, once again exactly like me.

We're Santangelos. We get it.

~ ~ ~

The three of us at dinner is surprisingly pleasant. Me, Dario, and Gino. A family unit.

You see, Daddy, I really don't need another family.

Gino is in a talkative mood, regaling us with stories about his early days in New York, the foster homes he'd been shuttled back and forth from, his teenage life of poverty and petty crime. He makes it all sound exciting and interesting, although I know he'd experienced tough times after his mom ran off when he was only five, and his dad was an abusive felon. Uncle Costa had revealed Gino's story to me one day with the hope that it would make me "calm down."

After dinner, Gino announces that he has a surprise for me.

The three of us head to the front of the hotel, and parked there, to my utter delight, is a gleaming red Ferrari. The car of my dreams.

"Oh my *God!*" I exclaim. "Is it really mine?"

"All yours, kiddo," Gino says with a great big grin. "I'm arrangin' to have it shipped to Washington. It'll be there before you know it."

I am overcome with joy. A Ferrari. A *red* Ferrari. It's the car I've always coveted.

"Can I drive it?" I beg.

"Be my guest," Gino says, still beaming.

He throws me the keys. I hug him.

"Do I get a Ferrari when *I* get married?" Dario jokes.

"No," Gino responds. "You get the keys to the whole hotel."

Those words kind of take the shine off. A Ferrari or the hotel? Hey—I'm kind of thinking I would prefer the keys to the hotel. But I guess—for now—a Ferrari will have to do.

CHAPTER FIFTY-ONE

It's my wedding day. The sun is shining. It's Vegas and I am getting married. Raoul appears early, and before I know it the penthouse is filled with people. Aunt Jen is fussing around, there is a hairdresser and makeup artist, and a lanky photographer is catching casual shots, while several assistants are running back and forth.

Gino's bedroom door is tightly shut. Dario and Olympia have yet to appear.

I feel isolated, surrounded by a sea of strangers.

Today is the day. *The* day.

My stomach's performing cartwheels. My heart is beating slowly—or is it fast? I'm not so sure.

Gino emerges. Dario arrives. Olympia appears.

I sit in a chair in front of a mirror, watching as I am changed into the picture of what a bride is supposed to look like.

When the pros are finished I race into the bedroom,

wipe off the creepy low-key makeup, and do my own thing. Then I rough up my hair into its usual tumble of long dark curls, and finally I look like me again.

Dario slides into the bathroom and offers me a joint. I take a couple of drags.

Raoul is ready with the dress. I slip into it. It skims my body and makes me feel beautiful.

"You are a picture of luminosity, child," Raoul coos. "A vision of wildness."

I try to smile. My lips feel dry. My throat feels constricted.

Somebody hands me a bouquet of white flowers.

I don't want to carry a bouquet. I hand it back to them.

Then we all set off downstairs to the flower garden where the wedding is to take place.

We stand outside, waiting, waiting, until it's time.

We hear the music and Gino takes my arm.

Daddy Dearest. Gino the Ram.

I love him. I hate him.

What am I doing?

Am I seeking my freedom, or am I sealing my fate?

Who knows?

I certainly don't.

We start the long walk down the flower-covered aisle. Me and Gino. A matching pair.

I spot Marco. Our eyes meet for a split second. We connect. One day he will be mine, I know this to be a fact.

The adventure is beginning. Is it an adventure or the start of some bleak nightmare?

I am sixteen years old and I am taking a step that could turn out to be a disaster.

My arm shakes. Gino holds me tight.

What is he thinking?

What am I thinking?

Is this a huge mistake?

I will never be Mrs. Craven Richmond. In my head I will always be Lucky Santangelo. A free spirit. A strong independent woman.

Yes, I am Lucky Santangelo, and one day I am going to take over Gino's empire.

Only time will tell . . .